I Can't Drink Because I Vomit!

Short Stories

W. S. Drake

I'm Not a Drunk Because I Vomit

Why am I not a drunk? Well, it's not because I haven't tried. My delicate constitution can't take it. I puke my guts up and then get dry heaves. The last time this happened to me was 1983. I promised God that if I ever stopped vomiting, I would never, ever, ever, ever touch a drop of tequila again. And, I never have.

I'm Not a Drunk Because I got Busted

Why am I not a drunk? You could say I learned my lesson at 17. I had fake ID and joined my older brothers for a night of celebration after they won their hockey tournament. I got pretty relaxed after a few beers at the local watering hole and made nice with the guys competing in the darts competition. The bar closed early, as there was a storm on its way. I invited the guys to join my brothers and me at our house for pizza and a few more beers. Our parents were asleep, so I asked the new friends to tip toe up the back staircase where I led them to our secret garden in the attic. I rolled joints for my new friends who produced their FBI badges and the rest is history.

I'm Not a Drunk Because I Say Bad Stuff

Why am I not a drunk? Because, when I drink too much, I say what I really think. Like the time I genuflected in front of my mother-in-law and called her Holy Shit Face. She was horrified but my wife and father-in-law laughed, encouraged me and gave me my fourth martini. I was on a role. I then told my mother-in-law she was a sanctimonious bitch and that her ridiculously generous donations to the Church were wasted on the pedophile defense fund and certainly not going to feed the poor....and that her dollars wouldn't get her to Heaven....and then, my mother-in-law introduced me to the Bishop who had just arrived late for the dinner party.

Dear Readers,

My motivation for sharing these stories is my sincere hope
that you will see the many shades of substance use, from the
bright euphoria to the dark storm with deadly lightning
strikes. Addiction starts out on a high and ends with a
languishing low with nowhere to go but up to sobriety.

So, enjoy some laughs and perhaps shed a tear or two. If you
recognize yourself or anyone you might know, I assure you its
purely coincidental.

Being Irish and quite familiar with the use and abuse of
alcohol, I really can't drink because I vomit.

W. S. Drake

Table of Contents

Speak Easy

Becky paid her tuition on time without the help of student loans. She also paid for her younger sister's orthodontic work and her older brother's stint in rehab. But, no one in her family knew that she did so. The bills were paid anonymously.

Becky's parents were hard working folks who had a rough time of it when a bout with cancer took their life savings. But, that money was well spent as Becky won her battle with leukemia. She was only twelve and promised her parents that she would grow up to be rich and famous and buy a ranch and have horses.

This is how she did it. Becky talked trash and got paid very well for it. She had a voice that came to her through pain but provided her with promises fulfilled. It started out in the hospital, a most unlikely venue.

The nurses who helped her through the worst of the chemotherapy told her that all that retching would give her a gravely voice. "Drink tea with honey when you can get it down, dear," said Lucille, the duty nurse on the children's oncology floor.

Becky's doctor told her she sounded like a movie star from the 1940's when smoking was considered quite glamorous. It started out as a fun way to take Becky's mind off of how awful she felt. Doc said that there was a beautiful actress named Greta Garbo who loved to say, "Dahling, I vant to be alone." Becky hammed it up and said it whenever the IV had to be changed. She was good at imitating and often cheered her anguished mother with her impersonations of Hollywood's finest.

Becky recovered and graduated high school. She worked all summer to earn enough to attend Santa Barbara City College in the fall. She needed a part time job to pay for her expenses and found one purely by accident.

Becky was invited to do the bar crawl down State Street with some new friends. Becky wasn't much of a drinker but wanted to go along for the fun of it. The caveat for the drinkers was Becky as designated driver.

They started out at Joe's, a very popular spot with locals and tourists alike. They stayed a while as it was happy hour and the drinks were two for the price of one. Becky drank tonic and lime and started chatting with the bartender. He was a graduate student from the University of California at Santa Barbara. His name was Greg and he told Becky he was working tending bar to survive while he earned his masters in computer science. "So, Becky, what are you studying?" he asked.

"I'm taking the basics now in speech pathology," said Becky.

Greg and Becky chatted for a few minutes, till an older gentleman sat down and ordered a martini with extra olives. He couldn't take his eyes off Becky. Did I mention Becky was a tall blonde with piercing blue eyes and a surfer's body? Her hair was short and sassy, she wore minimal makeup and had an easy smile. The gent was smitten.

"So, Greg, who's the new kid in town?" he asked with a twinkle in his eye.

"Hey, Mr. Carmichael, meet Becky, the designated driver for her pals at City College."

Becky said hello and Jack Carmichael was hooked.

"Now, there's a voice! I could listen to you all night," he said. Becky was flattered and laughed and told Jack, "...but Dahling, I vant to be alone."

Jack nearly fell off his chair laughing. He asked Becky if she could carry on a conversation as Greta Garbo. "Yeah, I can do Greta all night long."

Jack ordered another martini. Becky kept in character and told Jack about her ambitions to help people with speech impediments and to someday have a ranch with horses. Jack told Becky that she could do anything she set her mind to. Becky, answered as Greta, " Dahling, do you really think so?"

Jack told her that she had a fabulous future and that the world awaited anyone willing to work hard. He asked her how she learned to talk as Greta. Becky told him she had been sick for a while and had watched old movies and then imitated the movie stars.

Jack finished his martini and popped a fifty to Greg, telling him to keep the change. He then took Becky's hand and popped a hundred in it and asked her to say goodbye as Greta.

"So long, Dahling."

Becky was thrilled. She had a hundred dollar bill just for being nice to a lonesome guy and doing her Greta voice. Greg said that Jack was a regular and he was one of the Montecito elite who had invested heavily in IBM decades ago. Greg told Becky she was on to something. Becky said she needed to make enough money for the following semester and wondered if bartending might work for her.

"It could, but why do this and stand on your feet all night?" asked Greg. "If were you, I'd get a 900 number and talk to dirty old men."

Becky laughed, "You're kidding, right?"

"Hell no," said Greg. "I'll join you and we can split the cost of the line, and the hours."

"Well, no one would know who we are," said Becky.

Greg asked Becky if she could do other voices. She gave him a sample of an innocent ingénue, a southern belle, and a Spanish Senorita. Becky could do accents, sweet nothings, nasty temper tantrums, and a sexy, "fuck me, please."

Greg said he could do Antonio Banderas, Nathan Lane and John Wayne. Between them, they had all the voices they needed to satisfy any horny guy or gal willing to pop a few bucks for a dirty call.

Becky and Greg made plans to meet at Hendry's Beach the following afternoon. They would each give it some thought and get a plan of action.

Becky biked over and met Greg for a long beach walk to Hope Ranch and back. They had each done some Google research and had the hard costs of setting up the line. Greg had his own studio apartment and could get the line set up there for privacy. With their school schedules, they decided on late night hours, from 9 pm to midnight. Greg would take Sunday, Tuesday, and Wednesday, and Becky would take

Monday, Thursday and Friday. Greg needed to keep his
bartending gig and Becky wanted to be free to socialize on
Saturday nights.

"So, Greg, how on earth do we advertise this," asked Becky.

"Personal ads on free websites and then we keep regular
customers happy." Becky asked him if he had ever done this
before.

"No, but one of my geek roommates freshman year ate up
his book money calling a porn line just about every day. He
went through pre-loaded cell phones like they were bags of
chips. The guy was into more than one service. That's what
broke his piggy bank."

Becky told Greg that with the range of voices they could do,
customers could have one stop shopping.

"We'll let callers think that there are several operators
working at our station. I can be different voices on different
nights and develop a faithful client list."

Becky and Greg agreed that nothing too kinky or weird
would ever be discussed, and certainly nothing sadistic or
criminal.

" I'm not looking to chat with serial killers or wife beaters or
guys liking pain," said Becky.

"We can block any calls that cross the line," said Greg.

"We gotta make sure that callers can't find out where we are
or who we are," said Becky.

Greg laughed and told Becky that he had been a sport hacker
since he was 14 and knew how to route the calls in a circuitous
puzzle.

"No worries there. The biggest challenge will be staying fresh
and interesting. Plus, we will get a lot of calls from the lonely
and bored. Got to keep the conversational ball moving at least
10 minutes or longer."

They watched the surfers for a bit and made plans to meet at
Radio Shack the following morning to get their set up supplies
that included a recording device. Greg said it was good
business to keep a log of the calls and to learn what worked
and what didn't. Greg also told Becky that he could reverse the
call and identify the caller if a situation developed. Becky's

initial investment was the hundred dollars Jack gave her. It bought her share of the equipment.

Becky worried that she didn't have enough experience to talk the talk that callers might want. But, Becky was not one to shy from a challenge. She would have to write some scripts and hope that she didn't burst out laughing at some of the situations she might encounter. To prepare, Becky biked over to the Paperback Exchange on Cliff Drive to purchase romance novels with steamy sections.

The first week was spent placing ads on free websites. To entice callers and to build their base, they offered the first three minutes free with the purchase of a block of calls. Becky told Greg of her insecurity over what to say to callers when she answered the call. Greg said it wasn't so much what she said, but how she said it. Becky developed a system of flattery, questions and reactionary comments.

On Monday evenings, Becky answered each call in a southern drawl, "Hi Baby, what's on your mind tonight?" If the caller spoke obscenely, she would threaten to hang up if he didn't speak like a gentleman. "Now Baby, y'all know that that kind of language hurts my feelings and I'm a lady of the utmost refinement. Now, why don't you tell me what y'all are wearing and I'll tell y'all what I'm wearing."

Then, if the caller didn't clean up his act, she would fake cry and say that she would continue only if the caller minded his manners. If the caller got ugly, she disconnected the call, as callers were initially charged for three minutes, and then by the minute for every second after.

Often, Becky would get calls from lonely guys who just wanted to gripe about the unfairness of life and the boring work they did to pay the bills. Becky would steer the conversation to something positive to look forward to, such as taking dance lessons or learning golf. These were the most lucrative calls as lonely guys tended to cling to a good listener.

Thursday's calls were done in her best accents. Friday was a potpourri of characters including Sarah Palin, Queen Elizabeth, and, of course, Greta.

Greg did well for the first few months but bowed out because of his studies. He had too much on his plate. Becky continued and soon made enough to get her own studio apartment. Greg sold her his share of the equipment and set up her phones and computer. It wasn't long before Becky had regular clientele. One of her best selling calls was merely reading passages from the romance novels. She was amazed at what people would pay her to read.

One guy loved *Gone With The Wind* and another was into *Tale of Two Cities*. There were others who wanted the steamy passages from *Fifty Shades of Grey*. Danielle Steele's books were a reliable source as well as Diana Gabaldon. She loved to moan, "Oh Jamie boy." For calls lasting 15 minutes or longer, Becky signed off with, "...call again sugar...you always get me at hello."

Becky got a call at 11:43 on a Sunday night in April. She was getting tired and looking forward to shutting down and getting a good night's sleep. The caller sounded drunk and told her that he had accidentally called a wrong number. She'd heard that line about a thousand times. Becky had answered as Greta. "Vhat, ever do you vant at this hour? You know I vant to be alone."

The caller stayed on the line. Becky recognized the voice and Jack recognized the perky blonde who could do a great Garbo. Becky was flustered as this was the unknowing investor in her successful home business. Plus, she was outed and so was he. Becky didn't buy the wrong number routine.

"Dahling, are you nibbling on those olives?" Becky asked.

"Yes, and they are delicious....soaked in gin."

Jack asked Becky to tell him about herself and if she was fond of mature men. "Dahling, I love a man who knows his way around the world and especially, my world."

Jack then asked, "Been to Joe's lately?" Becky answered, "No, how about you Mr. Carmichael?"

Well, there you have it! This was the beginning of Becky's new direction in life. She told Jack that she owed him a debt of gratitude as it all started with her fun evening doing Garbo. Jack was both horrified and delighted at this turn of events.

He scolded her for lowering herself to talk dirty to horny misfits, then said, "Jesus Christ Almighty! You don't have to stoop to this level. You got it all, smarts and looks. What the fuck are you doing with your life? If you were my daughter, I'd take you over my knee and spank you!"

"Oh Baby, you know I'd like that!"

They both cracked up and Jack said he needed to refresh his martini and get a few olives. Becky waited and the clock kept ticking. Calls after 11 pm were more expensive. Not a problem for Jack. He came back on the line and told Becky he was raising his glass to her and said, "Talk about an entrepreneur!" Becky said it paid her bills and she could still keep her grades up.

"Yeah, I bet you keep your callers 'up' too!"

More laughter. Then, reality set into Jack. He was a sterling member of the community, married with children and grandchildren. Becky had the goods on him. Jack was pissed at himself. He never used his home phone for trash talk. He only used a pre-paid cell phone and a pre-paid Master Card. Jack had been drinking way too much lately and this was his own stupid fault.

Jack asked Becky to meet him at Joe's for lunch the next day. She agreed. Somewhere between Jack's second Bloody Mary and Becky's second tonic and lime, they agreed upon a business plan that would provide Becky with a secure future and the ranch she always dreamed about.

"I need a promise from you Becky," said Jack.

"What's that Mr. Carmichael?"

"You will quit the calling business and use that education of yours."

"Why would I do that Mr. Carmichael?" asked Becky. "I've got student loans to pay off and my parents need help with my sister and brother. Horny jerk offs pay good money and I need it."

"Because, I will make it worth your while and then some," replied Jack. He proceeded to tell Becky that he owned a building on Coast Village Drive, the main drag of Montecito. He would set her up in a speech therapy business and give her a fifty year lease on a piece of land he owned in Carpinteria. He would invest in the business and be a silent partner. Jack also needed a tax deduction and would set up the 100 acres as a horse ranch where Veterans with post traumatic stress disorder could come and ride and help with ranch chores. Jack said he loved animals and would feel good about that kind of legacy for the community. Becky could live on the property. Jack would build a barn and a house.

Jack said he knew his drinking had gotten out of hand. He told Becky that he couldn't bear the thought of his family finding out about his secret chats.

Becky was no fool and accepted the offer. Jack was no fool and made her sign a confidentiality agreement at his attorney's office. Becky recognized the attorney's voice as the guy who called from his shower. Becky smiled and said as Blanche Dubois, "I could always use the ongoing help of another investor with a good legal mind."

The attorney bought Becky a string of mules from the rescue ranch in Bishop, California. Mules were the most sure-footed for trail riding. He also paid for the training of the grateful animals and set up ten acres for dog and cat rescue. It was a pleasure for him to do this as he quickly embraced the love of animals. He and a bunch of his new pals at AA went to the ranch every Saturday morning for their meeting in the barn that Jack built. Then, they did ranch chores and fed carrots to the mules and cleaned the kennels.

Altar Wine

Sheila McCarthy was one of those unfortunate people genetically predisposed to become a problem drinker. You might guess by her name that she was Irish. And, lord knows, if ever there was a culture made to drink, it was the Irish.

Sheila never sipped an alcoholic beverage that she didn't like, nor did she leave a drop in the glass. Baby boomers of the sixties knew better than to waste! Their parents and grandparents told horror stories of the Great Depression.

"If you knew the pain of hunger, you would never, ever throw food out!"

The lean years of the 1930's scarred and scared them for life, and, for better or worse, they guilt tripped their children, passing on the waste not, want not way of life. No vegetable, no piece of meat, salad, fruit, bread or beverage was left unconsumed. If there were leftovers, they appeared in all manner of casseroles, infused with the spices in the cupboard to make them palatable.

Canned tomatoes, chopped onions, garlic cloves and a man sized hunk of Velveeta could transform Sunday's family supper to Wednesday's wonder meal, presented in a large Pyrex baking dish. Everything was in that dish! Stale bread was slapped on the bottom, and whatever was left in the refrigerator was layered like hodgepodge lasagna and topped off with stale chips, a few quirts of olive oil and plenty of salt. Boomers ate it and it wasn't too bad if there were enough chips on top to soak up the Velveeta.

The same philosophy was applied to alcohol. Never, ever, ever waste a drop! Sheila McCarthy got the message.

"Good booze and good beer cost damn good, hard earned money," said Gramps as he drained what was left of Gram's whiskey sour. That, of course, was on top of his glass of Canadian Club on the rocks with his beer chaser. Sheila heard the stories over and over again of how tough it was in the 1930's. Everyone had a vegetable garden and shared with their neighbors. They also shared their hooch and coveted every drop. "Bottoms Up!" "Don't throw that out, I'll drink it!"

It actually started a bit before the Great Depression, when street cops and G-Men had nothing better to do than to enforce the craziness of Prohibition, which made criminals out of most red-blooded normal folks as they made their own and shared that too.

Sheila was fascinated with the talk of the roaring twenties when Gramps made corn "licker" and what they referred to as "exciting apple cider." His brother Harold was the beer man and Gram could take any kind of berries and make special dessert sauce for homemade ice cream, which was just as tasty out of the glass, and the bonus was that it could turn a frown upside down.

The high quality stuff came over the river from Canada. Sheila's Canadian relatives and her grandparents had a second career as bootleggers. Every family get together was an excuse for a little business. Gram's brother George would go fishing throughout the spring, summer and fall, coming across the St. Clair River from Walpole Island. He usually stayed for a few days. He crossed at three in the morning if the weather was good. Gramps met him in Algonac and they loaded the booze into his car. Gram drove home and stashed it in the root cellar along side the potatoes, beets, carrots and squash. Gramps got in the boat with Uncle George and they fished till about noon, when Gram came to pick them up.

The law enforcement was more active at the Windsor-Detroit border and lacked the staff to patrol every little island throughout the scenic route from Lake St. Clair to the St. Clair River and Straights, leading to the mouth of Lake Huron.

Parties were a way of life for Sheila's Irish family. They brought out the good silver and crystal on birthdays, Christmas, Easter Sunday, 4th of July and the most wonderful celebration of all, St Patrick's Day.

March 17, 1959 was one hell of a party! For Sheila, it was the beginning of her relationship with alcohol. She was nine years old, precocious and the youngest of the McCarthy family. The day started off with the entire family attending Mass at St.

Kevin's Catholic Church. Monsignor Sullivan said the Mass and stayed for the potato pancake breakfast that followed. The children's choir sang at the Mass and entertained at the breakfast. Irish coffee was served with the pancakes. In attendance were the businessmen, judges, policemen, lawyers, architects, plumbers, barbers and anyone who was Irish or wanted to be who could get the day off or get conveniently sick that morning.

By noon, the crowd moved to the Irish Club. Before lunch was served, speakers from the Irish Genealogical Society gave interesting talks on Irish history, never sparing the English and their cruelty to the Irish. Monsignor Sullivan was only too cognizant of the fact that several of his faithful were in cahoots with the Irish Republican Army. He was off the hook however, as he was under the seal of Confession.

Lunch was Shepherd's pie and Irish Soda Bread. Green beer kept the crowd lively. By the time the corned beef and cabbage supper was served several hours later, the non- Irish could hear the music and stomping of the step dancers from their homes. The club closed at 10 pm and the families went to their homes to continue the celebration or to pass out.

Sheila was a light sleeper and got up to see what was going on downstairs. What she saw was way too much fun for her to miss. Her dad was playing the piano and the uncles were singing *McNamara's Band.* Some of them were crying when they got to the ballads, *Too Ra Loo Ra Loo Ra,* and *When Irish Eyes Are Smiling.*

Sheila had school the next day and was up before her parents. She went downstairs and saw several unfinished glasses of *Bushmill's Irish Whiskey* and green beer. She took a sip of the whiskey and found it a bit like medicine. So, creative Sheila put a teaspoon of sugar in it and did the bottoms up. The beer was tasty, even warm and she bottoms upped that too. Being a good little helper, she put the glasses and dishes in the kitchen sink. She got dressed and woke her mother up to kiss her goodbye. She had brushed her teeth and was chewing gum, not that her mother would have noticed. Sheila was a little buzzed and she liked it.

Being a people pleaser, Sheila eagerly helped her Mother in the kitchen and enjoyed the role of server for all the dinner parties and family gatherings. She learned to serve on the left and take from the right and to pour the adult beverages with care. No one noticed a few sips here and there from the kitchen before and after serving. For her efforts, Sheila was paid a dollar and treated to a double dipper ice cream cone at 31 Flavors the following day.

Time passed and Sheila became a fun adolescent and closet drinker. She learned to make *Jell-O* with vodka, careful to put the vodka in only her bowl of *Jell-O*. Sheila's mother was proud of Sheila, telling everyone how much help she was in the kitchen.

"Sheila makes Jell-O salad a few times every week and on the weekends, she is always up before anyone and surprises me with a tidied up living room and spotless kitchen. And she is such a darling with her chores! She has never broken a single Waterford whiskey or wine glass!"

Sheila grew into a beautiful teenager and loved to be the center of attention. Alcohol fueled her performances. She faithfully watched *American Bandstand* and practiced the dance steps that she saw on the TV. That girl could dance the twist, the mashed potato and the dirty boogie, the latter of which got her noticed by boys a bit older than she. Every other Saturday, the Mom's Club from Dominican High School and the Dad's Club from Notre Dame Academy put together a sock hop in the school gymnasiums, alternating schools.

It was at one of the sock hops that Sheila caught the eye of Joe Morelli, the dreamboat of the senior class, as well as Father Melvin Tucker, the geometry and calculus teacher. Friar Tuck, as the boys called him, watched in horror and secret delight as Sheila did the shimmy to *California Sun* and then locked herself to Joe's groin as they danced to *Misty* by Johnny Mathis. Tuck knew he should break them up but he was enjoying the scene and vicariously stimulated by the horny teens. The chaperoning parents were also dancing and didn't seem to notice.

After a few of these sock hops, Sheila and Joe were making out at every chance they got. Joe's parents were wine drinkers, being Italian and all. Joe had developed a taste for port, as he liked the sweetness. Sheila, by this time was 15, a sophomore and not particular about what she drank. As long as she got a buzz, she was a happy girl. Joe kept a mason jar filled with port in the glove box of his VW Beetle and shared it eagerly with Sheila.

Joe was a healthy, red-blooded boy, and, although he enjoyed rock n roll dancing at the gym with Sheila, all he could think about was the horizontal mambo. Sheila was a 15-year-old closet boozer with raging hormones. She dreamt of going steady with Joe and being the envy of her classmates. Joe was considered the best catch at Notre Dame Academy as he was not only gorgeous but also kind hearted, fun and he could dance.

It was the 60's and the nuns did their job on presenting sexual activity of any kind to be hell worthy. Joe knew this and had convinced Sheila that French kissing was not an imitation of intercourse with tongues and certainly not a mortal sin. He tried the traveling hands routine, but could only get to nearly second base with Sheila before fear and tears set in. Friar Tuck solved that problem. But first, a little background on Tuck, the chaperone of choice.

He was a handsome six feet and taught martial arts in addition to geometry and calculus. He could easily break up any fights that broke out, but nine times out of ten, he used his powers of persuasion to talk with the troublemakers and convince them to behave. Tuck was a fun guy who loved music and brought his collection of albums to the sock hops. He was really into Motown and got all the wallflowers on the floor with his teaching of the electric slide. He made everyone laugh as he pulled the hood on and lifted the hem of his cassock while showing the students the steps. In addition, he was easy on the eyes and had a neatly trimmed beard. So, what was hell was he doing in the priesthood?

Joe idolized Friar Tuck and craved his approval. Joe had a strained relationship with his father and Tuck seemed to fill the void. Tuck gave Joe plenty of approval as Joe aced his geometry and calculus classes and shared his love of music. Joe told Tuck that he was quite fond of Sheila and that Sheila was a virgin. He wanted to be her first but was experiencing the Catholic guilt trip, or the ultimate mind fuck as it was so eloquently referred to by his classmates.

Joe told Tuck that he envisioned a future with Sheila as his wife. Tuck said to be gentle with Sheila and offered to speak to her. Tuck counseled Joe that teen-age girls were very sensitive about these matters.

To complicate things even more, Joe was being groomed for the family business. His father, Augustus Vincent Morelli wanted Joe to go to law school and become the family consigliore. Big Gus was quite successful in waste management and owned a chain of Italian Restaurants. Gus was an active member of the Knights of Columbus and a big donor to all Catholic charities. He was on the list of wise guys that the FBI watched but skillfully ran his businesses and paid for apathy.

Big Gus loved the Sunday afternoon family meals at his restaurants and encouraged family members to bring guests, especially if his cousin Gina was doing the cooking. Gina inherited their grandmother's cookbooks and followed each recipe to a *t* using the best of the imported extra virgin olive oil, the farmer's market fresh vegetables and plenty of garlic.

Joe brought Sheila to Sunday dinner at *Gustavo's* in early May. He planned on asking Sheila to the senior prom and thought that the timing would be perfect after the tiramisu dessert. Sheila wore her best dress and Poppagallo flats and borrowed her mother's pearls. She looked lovely, but not at all Italian. Did I mention that Sheila had piercing green eyes and strawberry blond hair?

Gus thought Sheila was a knock out, charming and a real sweetie. She loved the lasagna and told Gus that her parents allowed her to drink wine with her meals. She had two glasses of Chianti and cleaned her plate. Gus told Joe in the men's room that this was only a fling and not to get serious as no son of his would ever permanently hook up with anyone not

Italian. In fact, Gus and Jack Rubio had seriously discussed a merger after Joe finished law school. Annette Rubio was a few years younger and would make a good wife for Joe. Rubio Construction was a potential client for Joe's future law firm.

Joe was pissed at his father but said nothing. He drove Sheila home. Between long and wet kisses, he asked her to accompany him to the senior prom. She accepted. Sheila went into the house and gleefully told her family that she had a date for the Notre Dame Academy senior prom. It was five o'clock and her parents were enjoying gin and tonics while the leg of lamb was roasting in the oven. Sheila said she would get a glass of ginger ale and join them and they could discuss prom dresses, shoes and how to style her hair. She was so excited. Sheila's parents never knew she popped a healthy shot of gin in her ginger ale.

The prom was three weeks away. Sheila could hardly wait. Her dress was a cornflower blue with spaghetti straps. The shoes were dyed blue and had a safe, one-inch heel that would not interfere with dancing. Her wrap was a white silk stole with embroidered cornflower blue flowers. Sheila was falling madly in love and lust with Joe and was so proud of herself for landing the best looking guy at Notre Dame Academy as her prom date. In her mind, it was like a wedding day. Sheila was sure that he would ask her to go steady that night.

Joe followed up on Friar Tuck's suggestion and asked Sheila to meet with him. Tuck met Sheila in the sacristy after Saturday morning mass. He told her that she could confide in him and that he wanted to be her friend as she maneuvered the many issues facing teen-agers in love. Tuck saw that Sheila was nervous and offered her a chalice of altar wine. She drank it down like a glass of milk.

Through her tears, Sheila said she was grateful for the meeting and told Friar Tuck that she thought of sex a lot and wanted to experience this with Joe but was afraid. Tuck told her that she was a child of God and that God made her in his image and likeness and sexual urges were part of being a child of God. He then hugged her, holding her close, letting her sob.

Tuck told Sheila that he too was a child of God and had the same urges. He told her that she could release her anxieties with him at anytime. His hands lingered a bit on her back and he became aroused as he pushed himself against her. Sheila was a little bit buzzed and barely noticed the aggression. Tuck told Sheila to meet with him again on Thursday, following the late afternoon confessions.

The Prom was that night. Sheila looked beautiful and Joe looked handsome. The Notre Dame Academy Gym was transformed to replicate American Bandstand. One of the parental chaperones played the role of Dick Clark. The attendees had three hours of dancing to the Beatles, Jan and Dean, Connie Frances, Frankie Avalon, The Temptations and The Four Tops.

Sheila and Joe left before the Prom was over so they could have some special time alone. With plenty of port to relax and ease the conscience, Sheila let Joe get to second base. It was wonderful and Joe came into his own as they went from light to heavy petting.

Sheila was upset as she thought it was all her fault and the nuns were right! Boys couldn't help themselves and girls were on the hook as daughters of Eve, the temptress of all time!

Joe told her he loved her and she told him she loved him. Sheila said she needed to talk to Friar Tuck and would go to Confession to him on Thursday. Sheila told her parents that she was meeting friends at the library to work on her history assignment and that she would be home by 7 pm.

At confession, Sheila whispered her usual sins of disobedience, impatience and unkindness, saving the worst for last. She started crying. "Friar Tuck, it's me, Sheila. I'm going to hell for sure cause Joe wet himself and its all my fault!"

The compassionate Friar Tuck told her that she wasn't going to hell and to say a decade of the Rosary and to meet him in the sacristy after confessions were over. She did and he gave her a chalice of altar wine to calm down, repeating his talk of being a child of God and that male bodily functions were just a way of life. Sheila gulped her wine and began to cry.

Tuck hugged her close and let her sob. He then poured himself a chalice of altar wine and gave another to Sheila, who by this time, felt warm and safe and let Friar Tuck hold her very close. He too, came into his own and told Sheila that this was just part of God's natural plan and that if the heart was pure, then, it wasn't a sin. Friar Tuck told Sheila that they should meet every Thursday after Confessions and she could pour her heart out and get priestly guidance.

Sheila was both confused and thrilled to hear that she wasn't going to hell. The following Saturday, Joe and Sheila joined their friends in working on the Notre Dame Academy Year Book. When Joe drove Sheila home that night, he noticed that her parents were not yet home from their potluck down the street. They each guzzled some port and decided to watch Johnny Carson for a bit. Joe could still make his curfew. Sheila said her parents would probably not be home for an hour or so.

Joe turned on the television while Sheila went to the kitchen to get pretzels and two Cokes with generous shots of rum. Her parents didn't monitor the liquor cabinet and Sheila was careful to vary her sips. Kissing was good but bonus petting was even better. Joe came into his own again.

Sheila kissed Joe goodnight at 11:45 and had another shot of rum. Joe was crazed with desire and called Sheila the next day, asking her to meet him at the library at 4 pm. He told his father that he couldn't attend Sunday afternoon dinner with the family, as he had to do research for his senior term paper.

Joe and Sheila met in the parking lot of the library and shared some port. He told her he wanted to marry her after college and that they needed to consummate their love. Sheila agreed. They would do the deed soon.

That Thursday, after Confession, Sheila met with Friar Tuck and told him Joe wanted to marry her after college. Tuck smiled and said they should toast young love and brought out the altar wine. Sheila had two chalices and was into her third when Tuck hugged her and said this was all part of the Divine Plan. His hands traveled up her skirt. Tuck whispered to Sheila, telling her what a sweet treasure she was, as he pulled her panties down. Sheila was confused. He brought her to his lap and unzipped his pants. It all happened so fast.

Sheila felt a sharp pain as Tuck rocked her vigorously. She began to cry and he said it was all part of nature and that tears were not part of the program. Men of God needed a release and she needed guidance. He only wanted to show her God's love. He zipped up and gave her a blessing. Sheila went home and took a bath. She ate little at dinner and after, while doing the dishes, snuck a glass of gin as her parents were watching Bonanza in the family room.

Joe had matinee tickets for Jesus Christ Super Star on Saturday afternoon. He borrowed his mother's Cadillac for the special occasion. He picked Sheila up at 1 pm and noticed that she was a bit distracted. He asked what was wrong and Sheila told him she was worried about final exams. She couldn't tell Joe what happened with Friar Tuck as she herself didn't understand it and her recollection was fuzzy.

Sheila enjoyed the musical and especially liked the song, *I Don't Know How To Love Him*. For two Catholic students, the story was one they knew. Andrew Lloyd Webber's genius made is real for them. They drove to Anchor Bay and parked the car behind the maintenance shed where no one would notice them.

Joe had the port in Coke bottles and they drank freely. Sheila had four small bottles of Dewar's Scotch from her father's airline collection and they drank those too. Making out with a buzz was terrific and the more Joe told Sheila that he loved her, the more aroused she became. The back seat was spacious enough for Joe and Sheila to lie down and progress to first, second, and third base. Joe was wild with his homerun fireworks and she was drunk.

A satisfied Joe realized that he needed to please Sheila. She didn't cry out as Joe had. Joe wanted to pleasure her and be her magical memory. They hugged for a while until he was ready again.

Sheila was sore, so Joe gave her another glass of port. He put her on top this time and they found their perfect rhythm. Sheila rocked and pumped and had her first orgasm.

Afterwards, Sheila was content in Joe's arms and didn't feel guilty. Why should she? Friar Tuck had told her it was all part of the Divine Plan. Sex was a beautiful thing and it felt good.

The following Thursday, Sheila dutifully went to Confession. Afterwards, she met with Friar Tuck in the sacristy. They drank altar wine and Tuck asked her to tell him all about it, sparing none of the details. Tuck told Sheila that pure love and the expression of it was not sinful. He poured them each another chalice of wine and said that he was proud of her for making Joe happy.

It was after the third chalice of wine that Tuck asked Sheila to kneel for a blessing. She did and he pushed her face to his unzipped pants. Sheila was tipsy and perplexed. As he recited the words in Latin, he pushed and gyrated against her. He brought her up to stand by him as he covered her mouth with his. Between long wet kisses, Tuck told her that she was part of God's plan to make him as happy as she made Joe.

Sheila was drunk and experiencing feelings of shame at her own arousal. But it was a beautiful thing and it felt good. Friar Tuck intertwined his tongue with hers, guiding her to a chair and placing her on his lap. She eagerly moved as Tuck pushed her hips with his strong hands. Tuck told her that God would bless her for making his priest as happy as Joe.

On the last Saturday of May, Sheila attended Joe's graduation ceremony from Notre Dame Academy. His parents had a party at *Gustavo's* and Sheila celebrated the occasion with plenty of wine. That night, they did it three times in the back of his mother's Cadillac.

Sheila's period should have started on June 5th. By June 15th, she was a little concerned. Friar Tuck was off on his yearly retreat and would not be back for two weeks. Sheila had no one to talk to but Joe. By the 4th of July, Sheila was panicked. Joe said it was probably just nerves and to just wait it out. By July 25th, Sheila knew she was pregnant. She was not quite 16 and although madly in love with Joe, couldn't be sure he was the father of her unborn child.

The situation was a nightmare. Sheila had morning sickness and although not showing, it was only a matter of time before her belly would give her away. She couldn't tell her mother or her father. They wouldn't understand. She definitely couldn't tell Joe about Friar Tuck. What if the child was his? Friar Tuck would be back on Friday, and soon she would ask his advice. Joe said he would come up with a plan.

On Saturday, Joe went to Confession and spilled his guts to Friar Tuck who said he would help. They met in the sacristy after Confessions concluded. Joe said he was terrified of his father and the mobsters and what they would do if he eloped with an underage girl, an Irish girl to boot. Tuck said he knew a man in Toledo who could help. He had some money he could lend to Joe and he could set it up. Joe was distraught with guilt and said he couldn't kill his baby. Tuck told him that there was more at stake here and that the greater good had to be preserved. Joe worried about Sheila and what this would do to her. Tuck said that God would give her strength. Joe agreed to follow Tuck's plan.

Sheila went to confession to Friar Tuck on Thursday as well and she too spilled her guts. Tuck met her in the Sacristy after Confessions concluded and gave her a chalice of altar wine as she cried over her predicament. Tuck joined her with a chalice and said that he had already talked it over with Joe and they would take care of everything. Not to worry, and have another chalice of wine to settle the nerves. Tuck told Sheila to go home as he had plans with the pastor for Bible study planning that night.

A week later, Sheila told her parents that she and Joe were meeting friends for a volley ball tournament and would be gone most of the day. She would call and let her mother know when she would be back home, depending on how the team played and if there was an extra game to break a tie.

Joe drove his VW to Toledo where they met Tuck's friend in the back room of a drug store. Sheila was terrified so Joe stayed with her and held her hand. It was awful.

Joe could not have imagined the reality of the speculum, the cutting and the blood. Sheila vomited after the fetus was disposed of in a plastic bag. She wore an extra pair of panties with her Kotex.

Sheila cried the entire drive back and said she felt dizzy. Joe gave her Coke and saltines. He felt badly for Sheila but greatly relieved of the burden. Sheila told her parents that she got hit with a ball on her head and was taking a couple of aspirins and going to bed early.

Three days later, Sheila's mother found her in a bloody bathtub, crying non-stop. Her temperature was 104 degrees. The doctor at the emergency room had seen this scenario before and asked to speak to Sheila alone. He asked her for the truth. She told him what happened. He told her that she would be all right, and that she would recover with antibiotics and rest. He also told her that by law, he had to tell her mother and to report the illegal abortion. Sheila became hysterical and had to be sedated.

Mrs. McCarthy promised her daughter that this experience would never be spoken of again, but Sheila had to stop seeing Joe and to start behaving like a good girl. Smart advice, as Joe would have the IRA to contend with if Barry McCarthy ever knew he was having sex with his teen-aged daughter.

Sheila never told her mother the entire truth. Just that she and Joe had done it once on Prom night and that he borrowed some money from a cousin to get the abortion. Sheila never went to Thursday confession again.

Joe went off to college and law school at Georgetown University in Washington, D.C. He eventually married Annette Rubio and had a prosperous career as a corporate attorney.

Friar Tuck traveled to Rome to study for his doctorate in comparative religions. Upon returning to the states, he became the pastor of a wealthy parish in Pittsburgh and eventually became a bishop.

Sheila continued to sneak hooch throughout the rest of high school, and then went wild in college. She was a full- blown alcoholic by 19. She drank to kill the hangovers and to stop the shakes. She liked sex, was on the pill and gave herself to those who wanted her.

The Saturday before Thanksgiving, Sheila drank beer at a fraternity party and popped a few tequila shots with it. She had developed quite a tolerance for alcohol by this time. It took a bit more for her to get buzzed. One of the frat boys offered her a pill that would make sex really, really great.

Sheila took one and washed it down with a jelly glass of tequila and a few pulls of a Corona. Sheila and the Frat boy enjoyed their romp and then smoked a joint while further enjoying the afterglow. They fell asleep. The last of the joint smoldered in the sheets, which caught fire. The Frat boy died a week later. Sheila was on top and dead when the firemen put the blaze out.

Vodka Man

Stanislaw Zamoyski liked vodka. He also liked horses, beautiful women and a good strong smoke with his favorite pipe, the one that he stole from one of his Nazi captors in 1943. Stanislaw's survival story was always better told if he and his audience were drinking vodka. He made sure of that. Stan still got worked up and red in the face with the telling of how he came to America and became the dressage trainer for the wealthy horse set in Boston.

I heard the story thirty years ago when I stabled my thoroughbred gelding at the 100 acre horse farm where Stan taught the basics of dressage, right on to the level required to compete in the Olympics. My horse and lessons were a bribe from my ex-husband. I had threatened to divorce him if he didn't seek treatment for his dramatic mood swings and violent behavior.

My ex was the star litigation attorney at a boutique law firm. A divorce mid career was not on his agenda. The horse and I fell in love at first sight. I put my divorce proceedings on hold and eagerly embraced the challenge of learning dressage.

I had heard the rumors about Stan. Rich and bored housewives flocked to his classes and some were known to kiss and tell of his many talents. In the equestrian community, Stan was known as a superb horseman who could make a horse and rider perform like ballroom dancers. Students of the Zamoyski Dressage Academy paid to be worked like boot camp and scolded harshly in front of their peers. The classes were limited to four riders in the dressage ring.

During the winter months, rodeo competitors and wranglers took lessons from Stan. Now that made an interesting dynamic! The cowboys brought their Quarter Horses in and left their spurs in their pick-ups. Stan told them if they learned to ride, they would never need spurs nor would they ever need a harsh bit. Spitting Skol in Stan's dressage arena was a sin not easily forgiven.

The cowboys cursed Stan under their breath but did as they were told. Stan bragged all summer as with each rodeo on the western circuit, his students made the big bucks. Several of his cowboys made it to the movies as skilled riders in the westerns.

Stan insisted on proper attire and proper grooming of both horse and rider. Lesson days were always an equine and rider fashion show. Stan was old school and by the book. No one entered the riding arena without polished boots, clean britches, velvet riding hat and leather gloves. God forbid if the saddle wasn't clean and smelling of Lexol! In his thick accent, Stan would shout and curse at any rider who didn't respect his rules. On top of that, he would demand a bottle of vodka from any rider who fell off, got bucked off or started to cry during his lessons.

I bought Stan a quart of vodka after I fell off trying desperately to do a flying lead change. My horse went left and I went right. I got the wind knocked out of me and could have broken my neck for all Stan cared. He just yelled "vokda!"

I got back on the horse, did my lead change correctly and was grateful the lesson was nearly over. I was pissed and didn't want to buy him his bottle, but I did, as I knew I wanted to finish the year of dressage training. I showed up at 5 pm with a quart of vodka in a brown paper bag. Stan invited me into his office and asked Donald, his star student whom he was grooming for the U.S. Equestrian Team to join us for a sip. After Stan had a few sips, Donald coaxed him into telling the story of how he wound up in Massachusetts.

Stan told us that he came to America to start a new life and to forget his old life what had been both a dream and a nightmare.

Stan was married to Marysia, the love of his life and living in Western Poland on a small farm. They had one child, a six-year old boy. Stan raised horses and sold them to wealthy Europeans. He also trained a few Europeans for dressage competitions. They were happy and life was good. Their son, young Kazimierz was the apple of his father's eye.

The nightmare began when the Nazi's invaded Poland and burned Stan's farm to the ground. His wife and son perished in the blaze. The Nazis took his horses for their SS Cavalry Brigade.

Stan was in Warsaw visiting his ailing parents and on the return trip back to his village when the train was stopped. All the men were taken off as prisoners of war. The women and children ran. Some made it to the forest. The others were shot.

Stan spoke both Polish and German and heard his captors talking about the villages that they had leveled. His was one of them. The Nazis boasted of taking the spoils, including the beautiful stallion at the horse farm near the border. There was only one and it was Stan's. They spoke of having their way with the beautiful woman at the farm house while her child looked on, and then of setting fire to the house.

I was horrified at what I was hearing. Stan drank more vodka and tears streamed down his face. He then told of how he was forced to help dig the body pit, where the prisoners dug their own mass grave and then lined up so that they fell into the pit when shot, one after the other. Stan was next to be shot when he heard one of the Nazi officers shout, "Stop....I think this man is Zamoyski."

When asked who Zamoyski was, the officer said that he was the horse trainer and that they could use him with the horses. "Don't shoot him and waste his ability."

Stan was made to work with horses for the rest of the war. He tended to their needs and was forced to train the Nazis to ride with skill. When victory in Europe finally came and he was liberated, Stan set out on foot for Vienna. He was determined to find the wealthy aristocrat whom he sold horses to.

Stan remembered the way to the horse farm but hardly recognized it after the years of Hitler's rule. Stan became a farm hand, repairing what was left of a once magnificent estate. He married Fredericka the kitchen maid and they had a son they named Boris. Fredericka was a Polish opera singer from Warsaw. She was in Vienna performing in a concert when Poland was invaded. She never saw her family again. Her hosts in Vienna saved her by giving her the position of kitchen maid and chief cook.

Fredericka was as beautiful as Stan was handsome. Theirs was a marriage born out of lust and convenience. Neither understood the toll the war had taken on the other. They were each grateful not to be alone, to have food and shelter and hope for the future.

Stan's skills in horse breeding and horse training were once again realized during the next ten years as Europe rebounded. He trained the horse and rider who won the dressage competition in Madrid in 1955. It was there that Charles Leahy met Stan and offered him a job. After maneuvering through the paperwork necessary to get visas and passports, Leahy brought Stan to Boston in 1958 and gave him his assignment to "get Bostonians on the U.S. Equestrian Team."

Stan, Fredericka and Boris became U.S. citizens. They had a small house on the Leahy estate and life got a lot better. Fredericka and Boris joined Stan in learning English from a tutor that Leahy hired. They each spoke German, Polish and French and were soon proficient in English. Fredericka became a tutor herself, helping students from the Boston International School with their language studies.

Prior to the war, Fredericka studied mathematics, art history and music at the University of Warsaw. She was well liked by her language students and often helped them with geometry and music. Fredericka also earned a little extra money by giving singing lessons. She was every inch a lady and tried to compensate for her husband's often crude and dispassionate ways.

Young Boris was adored by his mother and ignored by his father. Boris was smart and eager to please. He did well in school and excelled in any sport he tried. Mediocrity was not an option in any kind of physical activity. His father was a tough taskmaster and Boris couldn't disappoint his father. After all, he was the second son and had to compete with the memory of Kazimierz.

Stan rarely missed an opportunity to remind Boris that he could never replace Kaz, nor could he exceed any expectation Stan had for Kaz. Stan's bitterness worsened with time, always fueled by a night of drinking. Boris loved his father but also hated him.

Boris grew up with horses and could do anything his father could do. By the age of 14, Boris won every blue ribbon available for his age group in not only dressage but also jumping and vaulting. Stan was pleased with his son's performance but couldn't praise him. In his tortured mind, Stan felt that he was being unfaithful to Kaz.

Boris was now called Bob by his friends. Bob played basketball throughout high school and earned his letter sweater in junior year. Fredericka came to every basketball game and every horse show. Stan didn't much care for basketball and never came to a game. He pushed his son in any equestrian endeavor and used him for the barn chores.

Stan told Bob that the blue ribbons didn't give him any privileges and that hauling hay bales and cleaning stalls would make a man out of him. When students just couldn't get the hang of a pirouette or a lead change, Bob would be summoned to demonstrate. He was flawless.

On the days when Stan was hung over, Bob taught the lessons and handled all barn operations. The horses and the students loved him, as unlike Stan, Bob never raised his voice. He was persistent with his teaching and established himself as the boss without scaring the shit out of the horse and rider.

There were many occasions when Bob would appear after our lessons with Stan. Bob knew he could help us with demonstrating what Stan shouted about. In ten minutes, Bob had us up to class speed. He knew where to put the pressure on the horse with the knee, the toe, the thigh and how to draw the horse into the bit without yanking on the mouth. He also praised the horse in French, cooing "c'est bon."

Bob pretended he was the horse and had us interlock cupped hands so we could feel the right amount of subtle direction to put on our reins. Then, Bob would get on a horse and show us where to put our butts in the saddle and how to develop a proper riding seat. What he didn't do was yell at us as Stan did, "Sit the damn horse like you fucking it!"

My riding classmates and I loved Bob and told our friends about him. Bob started making extra money by sneaking off on his bike to other stables and giving lessons.

Bob turned 16 on May 1st. His birthday was celebrated by Fredericka with a cake with 16 candles and a small package that contained a leather key chain with keys to a Chevy pick-up truck. Fredericka had managed to save the $2,500 for the hardly used truck she bought from Mr. Leahy's gardener. Bob was ecstatic and said he would be getting his driver's license the following day.

Stan was furious, shouting that Bob would only get into trouble and that he had done nothing to deserve such a lavish gift.

Bob bought a trailer hitch so he could transport horses. One evening, the phone rang and Stan answered. It was one of his students asking for Bob. Stan was irked and asked why.

"Just need him to help us with the party next weekend," replied Laura Armstrong.

Bob heard his father talking and asked for the phone. Stan had been drinking vodka and was now into Schnapps with his dessert. Stan was angry and suspicious of what Bob might be contributing to a party.

Stan told Laura that Bob wasn't available. Bob was furious and told his father to mind his own business. Stan picked Bob up and threw him against the kitchen wall and began pounding his fallen son with his massive fists.

Fredericka tried to intervene and Stan hit her, and then shoved her face into the kitchen table. Fredericka was stunned and sobbing, begging her husband to stop.

There was a loud knock on the door. It was Elmer Stone, one of the wranglers who came to pay cash for his lessons. Fredericka ran to the door and screamed for Elmer to break up the fight. Elmer saw the blood on her face and her swelling eye. He also saw that Stan had a neck hold on his son and was pounding him with his fist.

Elmer was a bull rider. Not his style to hit women and kids. He walked over to Stan, kicked his legs out from under him and grabbed his hands from Bob's neck. Then he let loose with a few more kicks with his steel-toed boots, aptly placed at Stan's kidneys and ribs. The cracking sound accompanied Elmer's warning, "Hit Freddie and Bob again, you mother fuckin' prick and next time I'll break your goddamn neck."

Elmer took Fredericka to the emergency room. She was bruised and stressed out but otherwise OK. She wanted to return home but Bob said he would never walk into his father's house again. Stan was passed out on the couch when Fredericka returned and Elmer saw that she was safe for the moment. Bob said he would sleep in his truck and make sure that his mother was all right in the morning.

That weekend, Bob transported horses for the Boston Fillies Spring Ride and confided to Laura what had happened. Bob told her that he had walked out and would never stay under the same roof as his father. Laura hired Bob to work with her horses and to teach dressage to the Fillies. She gave him a small apartment in her stables so he could finish high school. Fredericka came to see him whenever she could.

Stan sank more and more into his vodka and passed out one night, neglecting to do his evening rounds at the barn. Fredericka was singing at a community concert and went straight to bed when she got home. Disgusted with Stan, she let him continue to sleep in his lazy boy chair.

The next morning, Stan walked down to the barn. It was smoldering and all the horses but one had died of smoke inhalation. Stan was drunk and didn't set the smoke alarms to ring at his house or at Leahy's. His pipe was found in the feed room.

Stan blamed his son who had left him. After all, it was his son's job to do nightly chores. Charles Leahy was devastated and fired Stan. Fredericka found a live-in position at a girl's boarding school and walked out on her abusive marriage.

Bob earned a scholarship to Holy Cross College in Worchester, Massachusetts. Laura's husband Leonard was an alumnus and wrote a glowing letter of recommendation. Bob was a whiz at languages and at mathematics thanks to Fredericka's support. While at Holy Cross, Bob met Ben Fairchild, the wealthy son of a real estate developer from New York. He invited Bob for Thanksgiving weekend.

Bob felt quite at home at the Fairchild Farm overlooking the Hudson River. Ben's father, Larry had ten horses and played polo. He was the patron of the Hudson Valley Polo Team. Unfortunately, Larry was the worst player on his team. Bob said he might be able to help. Somewhere between the turkey dinner and the plum pudding dessert, Bob explained to Larry that all horses would take direction and partner with their rider if given the right signals.

"It's all in the legs and the hands....basic dressage will help any kind of horse sport."

"So, tell me about yourself and how a macho guy like you rides the girly dressage stuff," laughed Larry.

Bob held court at the dining room table and gave the Fairchild family the quick recap of his relationship with horses, pointing out that even the rodeo wranglers benefit from dressage. Larry told Bob to get a good night's sleep and to meet him at the barn before breakfast.

Bob asked Larry to let him ride the least talented of his horses.

"Oh, that would be Daisy Mae, my bitchy mare with a mind of her own," said Larry.

Bob proceeded to shock and wow Larry and Ben and the farmhands by mounting Daisy bareback and making her fall in love with him. His gentle voice, skilled hands and legs gently persuaded the horse to move at his will.

"How the hell are you doing that," asked Larry.

"I think like a horse and then communicate with my body," said Bob.

This was the beginning of a very lucrative relationship for Bob. Larry hired him on the spot to teach him dressage. He jokingly asked Bob if he wanted to try polo. The answer was yes.

Bob graduated Magna Cum Laude from Holy Cross and for the next ten years, he played polo on the Hudson Valley Polo

Team. Larry gave him a position with his firm when Bob proposed to his youngest daughter.

Stan wallowed in self-pity till his savings were totally depleted. His only possession of value was his ability with horses. He eventually found work at a riding academy in Maine. He never contacted Fredericka or Bob again. He died a few years later of cirrhosis of the liver.

Fear of Punishment

Patrick Sanchez was born on March 17th in Pueblo, Colorado. His mother, Angelina was told by the doctor that her fifth child might come early. He calculated her due date, giving her a window from March 17th to March 25th. Angelina had selected names that corresponded to the feast days of the saints on the liturgical calendar. She hoped for a boy to arrive on the feast day of St. Joseph, March 19th.

Angelina and her husband, Enrique celebrated St. Patrick's Day with the Knights of Columbus. The corn beef and cabbage caused the worst gas Angelina had ever had in any of her pregnancies. That night, a nine-pound boy came into the world and was known from that day on as Patrick, the Irish one.

Patrick Sanchez was indeed an adorable baby. Very happy and always smiling, he learned his role in the family was to be that of an entertainer. Angelina delighted in teaching Patrick the Mariachi songs she grew up singing and the Irish tunes so popular on his special day. Angelina prompted Patrick to perform at every family and social gathering. His brothers and sisters doted on him as he was the last of the children to be born to Angelina and Enrique.

A fatal accident during an ice storm took Enrique when Patrick was still a baby. Enrique had mortgage insurance and a modest life insurance policy that kept Angelina and the children in their home but provided little else in the cost of raising and educating five children.

When Patrick was in the first grade, his music teacher took him under her wing. Mrs. Dominguez taught Patrick to use his diaphragm and how to breathe the way a singer should. By third grade, Patrick became her helper with chorale. Patrick had the gift of perfect pitch and eagerly helped his struggling classmates. His reward was free piano lessons. Patrick was a natural and quickly learned to read music and to play by ear.

Angelina worked cleaning houses and couldn't afford a piano at home, nor could she afford childcare for her youngest. An accommodation was made by the music teacher who kept Patrick with her till 5 pm during the school week. He had two hours after school Monday through Friday to finish his homework, play the school piano and to listen to Mrs. D's stories of the great music masters. She confided in Patrick that in addition to Beethoven and Bach, rockers Paul McCartney and Mick Jagger thrilled her to pieces.

By the time Patrick was in Middle School, he was playing in the school band and also making a little money at funerals. His sweet voice, starting to mature, was both heartbreaking and glorious as he sang the tearjerker, *On Eagle's Wings*. The Pastor at St. Mary's in Colorado Springs often sent for Patrick if there was a funeral for an Irish parishioner.

Patrick was known in the extended Catholic communities for his renditions of the Irish Ballads. Danny Boy got the crowd sobbing every time. The funerals paid a small stipend that Patrick dutifully gave to his mother. One year, the funeral money paid for sweaters, boots, jackets and mittens for the entire brood, bought at the Salvation Army Thrift Shop. Another year, the funeral pay was used for plumbing repairs. Patrick told Angelina that he would soon be a rock star and bring home the big bucks. He sang with the radio around the house and did Elvis impersonations.

Patrick's oldest sibling saw dollar signs. Maria Sanchez was working as a waitress at Hooters. Angelina didn't approve but Maria's tips were needed to help pay for the new roof. Maria was popular at Hooters and had eagerly embraced her opportunities that came from serving hot wings in barbecue sauce. The rockers who came in invited Maria to one of their gigs at a private party for a high school graduation. The band played it all from the Temptations to the Stones. Maria saw an opportunity for herself and her baby brother. She took her tips for the month and bought herself a pair of white knee high boots and very short shorts known as hot pants.

At the next invitation to a gig, Maria surprised the band with her spontaneous go-go dancing. The crowd loved it and Maria landed a lucrative part time job doing what she saw Goldie Hawn doing on Laugh-In. Once she was in the band, she brought her brother Patrick to band practice, telling the band members that she was babysitting and couldn't leave him home alone. Patrick could hit the high notes of *Little Deuce Coup* and blast away at *I Can't Get No Satisfaction*. The hip action and the "ah, thank you very much," sounded more like Elvis than Elvis. Patrick was twelve years old but with dark glasses he looked at least fifteen. Patrick asked if he could play a little on the keyboard when the band took a break. Patrick had the rock piano down pat, so to speak. The bandleader was impressed.

Soon, Maria and Patrick were performing on Friday and Saturday and the occasional Sunday afternoon. Angelina again looked the other way as the extra money came in. She even took a little of the money for upgrading her tequila, which she had well hidden in the back of the freezer, surrounded by two packages of Brussels sprouts which all the kids hated.

The band grew in popularity and Maria became known as Sexy Sanchez. She was soon performing dance solos while her brother Patrick sang *Little Egypt*, and *Lady Godiva*.

Maria's moves as a dancer were also put to very good use in other ways. Patrick accidentally walked in on his sister and a much older man at a gig while the band was on break. Maria had her legs wrapped around the guy whose pants were around his ankles. They were in a chair and Patrick couldn't believe his eyes. Being a good brother, Patrick tipped the chair over and started kicking the man. Maria was pissed and scolded him for ruining her lady thrill.

Patrick left immediately and went home. He walked in to find Angelina drinking her tequila straight up and looking at old photos of Enrique. Patrick was in a rage and Angelina gave him a glass of tequila to calm himself. He gulped it, coughed and then settled down. Patrick then poured his heart out to his mother. Angelina said that Maria had chili peppers in her pants. She hoped her oldest daughter's terrible example wouldn't affect the younger daughters who were in high school. Maria was hot to trot and it was worrisome to Angelina but she didn't know what to do about it.

Mother and son drank the entire bottle of cheap tequila. Patrick woke with a terrible headache and had to stay home from school. Angelina made herself throw up before she left for work and then forced down a piece of bread piled high with Jif Extra Crunchy. Protein and sugar seemed to do the trick for her. Patrick struggled to get his oatmeal down. That night, he saw Angelina replace the tequila in the freezer.

Patrick noticed his mother getting sadder around the holidays. She missed Enrique and stressed that she wasn't as good a mother as she should be. Her drinking became habitual and she couldn't hide it as well as she used to.

Angelina took the five kids to the parish hall for the Thanksgiving meal. She worked in the kitchen and volunteered her children to help with set up and clean up. The bonus being a wonderful turkey dinner with all the trimmings and plenty of leftovers for Angelina to take home. The meal was served at noon. By late afternoon, the crowd dispersed and the hall was spotless. The kids were anxious to get home and get out the Christmas decorations. Angelina had plenty of time to be sad and have a few shots before her sister Lupe came over with pumpkin pies and sopapillas.

Lupe was deeply religious and felt it was her duty to help her sister whenever she could. However, Lupe was bossy and critical. She was a passive aggressive bitty who bought the tolerance of her sister's family by showering them with gifts of food and occasionally a greeting card with McDonald's gift certificates. Lupe was nobody's fool and could always tell when Angelina was imbibing.

Right on schedule, Lupe showed up with dessert and attitude. Angelina was exhausted from her kitchen duties and was drinking her special lime aid when Lupe asked if she could have a sip. Angelina said she would pour her sister a glass, as she didn't want to spread germs. Lupe called her on the carpet and told her that she knew her juice was spiked and her drinking in front of her children was shameful.

Angelina was pissed. She pulled the tequila out of the freezer and said she would have another just to annoy Lupe.

This didn't sit well with Lupe who insisted that she not drink alone. Lupe and Angelina got roaring drunk. The kids were busy hauling Christmas decorations from the basement and making a complete mess of the kitchen. All four pies were devoured, leaving the undercooked and quite greasy sopapillas for the two sisters to munch on.

Angelina excused herself to use the bathroom. She really had to go and was also a bit queasy. Feeling the urge from both ends, she locked the door, as her condition wasn't worthy of an audience. With haste, she lifted the lid of the toilet and the Blessed Virgin Mary appeared to her, rising up from the waters.

There was no mistaking her for anyone else. She had the beautiful long flowing blue robe with a golden halo and stars all around it. Angelina was terrified and a bit confused with this vision at this time and place.

She blurted out a quick prayer, "Mary, Mother of God!" The Blessed Virgin Mary looked angrily down at Angelina and replied, "Yes, I am!" She was in no mood to placate a drunken Angelina.

The Blessed Virgin Mary pointed a finger at Angelina and sternly said, "If you don't stop your drinking, I will ask my son Jesus to make your daughters whores!" Angelina got on her knees and said, "I'll stop...please tell Jesus to forgive me."

With that the Blessed Virgin Mary smiled and disappeared. Angelina came back to the kitchen and made a pot of strong coffee. She poured the tequila down the drain and asked Lupe to join her in saying the rosary. Lupe asked why. Angelina told her sister that she needed forgiveness. Saying the rosary was good insurance.

Patrick Sanchez and his sister Maria became known as the Mexican Donny and Marie. They performed together for the next three years, making enough money to send Angelina and her daughters to beauty school and to open a shop. Patrick got a scholarship to Colorado State University in Fort Collins and became a psychologist, specializing in alcoholism. He told of Angelina's vision to only the most desperate of his patients.

The Winning Bid

"Ladies, who will start the bidding at $500 for this tall, handsome hunk of man," asked the auctioneer at the celebrity auction benefiting the Rocky Mountain Food Bank.

"He's tall, handsome and a winner in the courtroom and just about everywhere else."

Bradley Stockman stood on the platform and flashed his smile to the female audience. He felt foolish and secretly cursed his paralegal who had talked him into this farce. Brad would have gladly written a generous check to avoid this uncomfortable situation, but he owed a debt of gratitude to Lillian, his faithful assistant who had worked tirelessly on the last trial. Lillian, when not being a paralegal, volunteered at the Food Bank and helped organize the yearly fund-raiser.

"I see a raised paddle," cried the auctioneer. "There's another and another, and three more!"

The bidding went to $5,000. Brad was one of the most sought after bachelors in Denver. He stood six feet, had piercing blue eyes and looked fabulous in a suit, a tux and in his tennis whites. Brad was also the darling of the courts these days with a winning streak that belied the fiercest of jurists.

The competition settled among Christine Harden, a commercial real estate agent and the Assistant District Attorney, Gloria Delgado. Christine continued to bid beyond $3,000 and figured that Gloria was desperate when she trumped the bid by a thousand. Christine, a leggy blonde with curves was newly divorced and prepared to pay $4,000 for a date with Brad. It would be a grand entrance back into circulation. She decided to save her funds for the next bachelor, a pilot with Denver based Frontier Airlines. He was a dead ringer for Leonardo DiCaprio and was more her type.

"Five thousand, going once, going twice! Sold to Ms. Gloria Delgado!"

The room echoed with the thunderous claps of approval. This would be some date! The defense lawyer and the prosecutor! Bradley Stockman stepped down from the pedestal and into the arms of Gloria Delgado. Whispers among the jealous bidders included whether or not Brad was worth $5,000.

"He better be good in bed for five grand," whispered Christine. "Having TV cameras following around could spoil the romance if you ask me."

The high priced date included an afternoon playing golf at Arrowhead Golf Club in Littleton, followed by cocktails and dinner at The Palace Arms. The major sponsor of the Food Bank was the local ABC affiliate. The date would be featured on the news and in the society pages of the Denver Post. Great fodder for the journalists looking for human-interest stories.

Second generation Chicano, Gloria was born in Pueblo, Colorado to Jorge and Elizabeth Delgado. Gloria adored her Poppy and held all the men in her life to his seemingly impossible standards. In Gloria's mind, she wanted a guy like the one who married her mother, but with an education and money. Gloria was aware that they just don't make them like that anymore. At least not in her price range of professional, well to do men who exuded charm, sex appeal and devotion. Good luck Brad!

Gloria's grandparents on her father's side were migrant workers, originally from Chihuahua. Jorge was born in Brownsville, Texas in St. Mary's Hospital. He grew up with love and much hardship as he and his family depended on seasonal work in the fields and any kind of manual labor they could get in the off-season. Jorge lost both parents to cancer by the time he was 18. He blamed the pesticides they were constantly exposed to.

Jorge was strong, in body and in spirit. He spoke English and Spanish but never graduated from high school. Employment opportunities were limited. Jorge promised his mother on her deathbed that he would never work in the fields that killed her. He hated Brownsville and longed for four seasons and scenery that would make him glad to wake up in the morning. Shortly after his mother's pauper burial, Jorge hitchhiked to Colorado. The mountains welcomed him with their majestic snow capped vista. He breathed the cool air and knew he was home.

Jorge found the Salvation Army. They fed him and let him take a shower. He had a clean change of clothes with him in his sack. Jorge knew he could lift heavy things and his back was strong. The counselors at the Salvation Army helped him identify several local moving companies where he might be able to find work. Until then, Jorge said he could do anything that needed doing at the shelter, from cleaning to cooking to fixing things.

Lara Moving & Storage hired Jorge and put him to work in their warehouse. He did what he was told and never complained. This was his chance to escape the fields, to establish a home in Colorado, to experience a Rocky Mountain High that John Denver sang about.

Jorge married Elizabeth a year later. Baby Gloria came the following year. Jorge and Elizabeth had four more children. Without telling his devoutly Catholic wife, Jorge went to Planned Parenthood and got a vasectomy. He worked so hard to feed and shelter his family and more kids would kill them both.

Jorge wanted more for his five children and encouraged them to work hard in school and in everything in life. Jorge set an example by working two jobs, six days a week, leaving Sunday for family day. Gloria was the oldest and became her parent's helper early on. Jorge worked at Lara till four in the afternoon and cooked every evening at the local cantina. The moving work was hard and exhausting. Although still on his feet, the cooking was easy and he always brought home the food that would have been thrown out.

Gloria's mother, Elizabeth stayed home and raised her children. She brought in extra money by doing alterations for several clothing stores. Gloria learned to sew and learned to cook. She also made up her mind to become a super star in her family and in the Chicano community. She loved her family and was proud of her heritage. Yet, she longed for the respect shown to the courtroom attorneys she saw on the television screen. The actresses who played the parts wore such beautiful clothes, had their own trendy apartments in the city and for all Gloria could see, live glamorous lives. Nothing like the life she was living. Gloria shared her dreams with her parents.

"When I grow up, I wanna be a lawyer and put the bad guys in jail."

"Chica, to do that, you have to study so hard and get a scholarship. You know Momita and me no have money for college."

"No problem, Poppy. I can do it."

And she did. Little Gloria brought home stars on her work papers and regularly made the honor roll. Being the oldest, Gloria could change diapers, cook, clean and entertain kids. At twelve, she started babysitting for the Lara children. Jorge's boss had his hands full when his wife broke both legs in a ski accident in Vail. Jorge went to him and said he wanted to help. He brought Gloria to meet Mrs. Lara, who immediately loved this sweet and caring dynamo of a girl.

The Lara kids loved her even more. And why not? Gloria made them enchiladas, helped them with their homework, taught them some Spanish and played poker with them. She could do a mean poker face and showed them the art of bluffing. Gloria told them that playing cards was good for math skills.

Mrs. Lara recovered within a few months but found that she just couldn't imagine life without Gloria's help. So, everyday after school, Gloria rode the bus to the Lara house and performed the duties of a mother's helper. For both it was a win/win situation. Gloria was a godsend during the pandemonium time of children after school and before supper. Mrs. Lara made Gloria her pet project, teaching her the finer points of gracious living, from setting a formal dining table to dressing with style.

Every penny of her babysitting money went into her college fund in an old mayonnaise jar. When she saved up $500, Jorge took her into the local bank where she opened an interest bearing savings account. When he could, Jorge added to it, as did Elizabeth. Gloria's nest egg grew as she became the babysitter of choice for the well to do friends of the Laras. When not minding her charges, she tutored younger students in math and Spanish. Gloria was frugal. If she needed new shoes or clothes, she hit the thrift shops, looking for the best quality fabric and style. Wrong size? No problem as Elizabeth would re-make them to fit perfectly.

Gloria breezed through the SAT exam with the highest score among her classmates.

"Chica, you make us so proud," said Jorge.

With academic scholarships available at several universities, Gloria selected the one closest to home with a good pre law curriculum. She maintained straight A grades at Colorado College in Colorado Springs. When not in class, she worked as an assistant at a local law firm. Gloria graduated from the copy room to translating Spanish, both for witness interviews and for depositions.

Gloria heard about a poker game held after hours in the conference room. The buy-in was only $100 but as the night wore on, the stakes got mighty high. Gloria discretely inquired to one of the first year attorneys who told her that anyone with one hundred in cash could play.

"The game sometimes goes on all night," he said. "The biggest winner last month was the head of the patent and trademark office. The guy took the pot of ten grand. That's the limit."

Gloria showed up with her one hundred dollar bill and joined the game the following Friday. She won the ten thousand. The other players were astounded. Who was this pretty young thing and how could she do this? Easy. Gloria could read any tell on anyone, keep a perfect straight face and she could count cards.

She didn't play for a few months. Then, she did it again. She had enough to get a car and a better apartment off campus.

Gloria graduated Summa Cum Laude. She was the first in her family and in her neighborhood to achieve a college education. Jorge and Elizabeth cried with tears of joy as she received her diploma. Her brothers and sisters whistled and cheered for their big sister's success. Each promised her that they would also go to college and be something special in life.

Gloria was now a gorgeous Latin beauty. Raven haired with large brown eyes, she wore heels most days to add to her five feet four inches of height. Mrs. Lara wrote her a glowing letter of recommendation for the University of Denver Law School. With her grades and minority status, Gloria was awarded a substantial grant for her first year. She easily found a part time job at a full service law firm in downtown Denver.

Gloria played poker only when she really needed the extra cash. She didn't want to be known as a card shark. Her source of game locations was the personal ads on the internet. She drove to other states for the private games and always avoided the casinos, lest she be outed.

Gloria graduated Magna Cum Laude and passed the bar exam. She began her legal career at 25, and at the ripe old age of 33, she was well on her way to a political appointment. She put the bad guys in prison and felt good about it. But, her biological clock was ticking and it was time to find a husband.

Brad warmly returned Gloria's hug as the cameras flashed. It was all for charity and it would be great publicity. He told himself to laugh and enjoy the attention. It was just a date and Gloria was nice, pretty and smart as hell. He wouldn't be bored.

"Gloria! I didn't think you would bid on me! Will you ever forgive me for the Wilson trial?"

"Ancient history Brad. I do think however, that you were the eye candy for the jurors. Can't say I blame them!"

Brad and Gloria posed for the photographers. Gloria grinned as her credit card was swiped. She signed her name and flashed her receipt to the other bidders. The dream date was scheduled for the following Saturday.

Bradley Allen Stockman was the only child of Peter and Marion Stockman of Darien, Connecticut. Bradley grew up with most of the finer things in life. Every meal was served with Wedgwood China and silver flatware. The house Brad called home was a testimonial to the talents of the finest architects and designers. His clothes were preppy and his manners impeccable.

Young Brad played tennis, soccer, lacrosse and billiards. He took ballroom dance lessons at the country club and was a highly sought after escort for the debutantes. Money and privilege pretty much guaranteed that Brad would enjoy a charmed life.

Peter inherited big money, as did Marion. Other people managed it and each dabbled in real estate. Their investments did well, leaving them plenty of time for golf, partying and travel. Marion played the piano moderately well. Peter could carry a tune, and with a few drinks in him, he loudly accompanied Marion's show tunes and ballads. They were wonderful guests at dinner parties, even bringing along their Yamaha keyboard if the hosts didn't have a piano. Marion played at home on her Steinway Grand, a wedding gift from her parents. Brad took lessons at school and quickly decided that Billy Joel's music was much preferable to Beethoven.

Young Bradley was adorable and precocious. He had the best of au pairs from Europe and a private tutor. Parenting was kept at a minimum. Brad had plenty to occupy his time and plenty of people to keep an eye on him.

Education for young Brad began in the prestigious Montessori Preschool, ending at Harvard Law School. In between, Bradley excelled at his academics at private boarding schools, scored high points at every basketball game and earned the dubious reputation as not just the guy who could really drink, but also the guy who could hooch it from scratch.

Young Brad was the child of alcoholics and knew the finer points of booze, especially his mother's coveted recipe for homemade Kahlúa. Brad watched her it, and often helped by sampling it on vanilla ice cream. It was one of their favorite bonding experiences.

Brad had an itch that he couldn't scratch. He was anxious and never really satisfied with any high scoring game or straight A report card. He wanted more but couldn't really put his label on what he really wanted. Boredom was his worst nightmare. That all changed when he was 16.

The testing given to the students in the private high school that Brad attended, included psychological ones that projected paths in career choices. Brad was told by his counselor that he would make an excellent military leader, an excellent attorney, or perhaps an excellent architect. The tests showed Brad to be capable, creative and manipulative. The counselor knew that Brad liked to be the center of attention and seemed to crave a challenge. He encouraged him to look into a career in law. Brad was quite close to his counselor. He had a crush on him and craved his approval and bear hugs.

Brad did his undergraduate work at Dartmouth and went on to Harvard Law School. He studied hard and partied hard. Brad had a near perfect photographic memory, except when he drank to excess. His memory after drinking was as bad as his hangovers. As with most boozers, Brad was selective in what he could recall.

Brad only drank on the occasional weekend. He stayed focused on his goals and behaved like a boy scout while maintaining a 4.0 grade point average. But, when he drank, he drank a lot. Brad's charm got lost after a six-pack and tequila shots. It made Brad want to sin with anyone at any port in a storm. He wasn't selective and was known to lose all inhibitions. Rumor had it that he was the best ever for a threesome, and not opposed to two of his kind. It was said that he could go all night.

During law school, Brad worked part time for the University Alumni Association. He was good at fundraising, and the contacts he made were invaluable. He enjoyed a glass of wine with his evening meals but was careful not to pull any benders. One of the alumnus arranged for Brad to interview with Peabody Smithwick in Manhattan. Brad worked there for five years before coming to Denver. His exit from Manhattan was hasty.

Brad told his parents and co-workers that he was moving in a new direction and felt the call of the mountains. He opened up a one-man criminal defense firm and advertised heavily as the guy to call for help, whether guilty or not.

Brad's first year in Denver was lean as most of his clients were drunk drivers and deadbeat dads. He had the Yellow Pages and the late night television ads to thank for that. His big cases started to come in when one of his drunk driver clients recommended him to a friend, the friend being a wealthy Larimer Square bar owner caught cooking his books. Brad got him a sweet plea bargain deal, avoiding prison by paying the government ransom. Referrals poured in, and soon Brad had to hire an associate and a paralegal. Brad allowed himself only one drinking weekend a month to someplace he had never been to and always out of state. Too much was at stake in his new home city.

"Good Morning Gloria, this is Meg Wilson from Arrowhead Golf Club calling."

"Oh, hi. Are you calling to set up the tee time for Brad Stockman and me?"

"Yes, I have you scheduled for 9 this coming Saturday. Do you have your own clubs or do you need Arrowhead to provide them for you?"

"I have my own thanks. I've been playing for a few years now, and although I have never played at Arrowhead, I am eager to experience the challenge and the spectacular scenery. I just hope I can concentrate on my game!"

Gloria gave herself away. She was not just hinting at the magnificent giant red rocks throughout the golf course, but the nervous excitement of spending the day with Brad. The chatter about town included the possibility of a whirlwind romance and perhaps a wedding within the year.

Brad picked Gloria up just after 7. They stopped in Sedalia for coffee and croissants. Conversation was easy and they soon felt like old pals. Lawyers are like that. They rarely run out of things to say or to argue about.

Golf was pleasant and uneventful. The day was gorgeous and each was more impressed with the setting than with each other's skill at hitting the round ball. They enjoyed iced tea on the patio after nine holes and then decided to take a drive through Roxborough Park, the affluent residential area adjacent to Arrowhead.

"What a place to call home," said Gloria.

"If I were an architect, this is where I would want to get some assignments," said Brad.

"I second that," said Gloria "But, can you imagine the drive for people like us who work downtown? I wonder what the traffic is like on Santa Fe going downtown? You know, it never used to be like this. The DA has lived in Denver all his life and says he used to wear cowboy boots and his string tie to court in the 60's and 70's. Traffic was light and Denver was still a western cowboy town."

"Must have been fun in those days. I kinda like the Gerry Spense look myself, but I don't have the guts to wear my Davy Crockett jacket to court. Ha, can you imagine me switching my pin stripe navy blue Brooks Brothers for my rodeo attire?"

Gloria playfully poked Brad's arm and said, "I can see you in the cowboy swagger, a full 6 foot 4 in boots, roping in the jury! Who could resist you, even if your client was guilty as hell."

Dinner that night at the Palace Arms Restaurant was as good as it gets in Denver. They ordered the Chateaubriand and started with Oysters Rockefeller. They each had a glass of merlot. The photographers snapped their photo when Brad raised a glass to toast his lovely date.

Brad and Gloria easily talked about many things such as hiking a trail on Mt. Evans, the nastiest judge ever encountered, favorite books and the music they listened to on the radio. Dessert was chocolate mousse with coconut macaroons. The evening was lovely. Gloria was smitten with the dreamboat attorney.

The next few weeks found Brad and Gloria taking in the occasional lunch and finding a few hours on the weekend. Each was busy with work. They had an early movie night and Brad had tenderly kissed Gloria good night. Gloria told him that she could get use to it. They planned a ski trip for December once their work schedules could permit a four-day weekend.

Brad enjoyed Gloria's legal mind and took an interest in her upcoming murder trial. For Gloria, it was prosecutorial heaven as the high profile case was gruesome, sure to be on the daily pages of the Denver Post.

The hate crime involved the beating and castrating of a male prostitute. The accused was fresh out of the military, having served two tours of duty in Iraq. The prostitute was left for dead by the dumpster, outside an upscale eatery in LODO, the trendy lower downtown section of Denver. Other patrons of the dining establishment saw his slumped body and called 911. The victim lived but lost what was once his tool package for his trade.

Gloria confided to Brad that she was both excited about such a trial but terrified that she not make any crucial mistakes. The evidence was there but the accused was a decorated soldier with no criminal record or stain on his military service. Great exposure for Gloria as she lobbied for her political advancement but the pressure was on and Gloria was nervous. She needed the jury to listen to her, to love her and to be convinced by her presentation of the facts. It was the beyond the shadow of doubt clause that worried her.

"I've got a few years of criminal defense under my belt," said Brad. "You can pick my brain. I'll try and come in for opening arguments and some of the key witness questioning."

"Oh Brad," said Gloria. "That would be great. I have so much at stake with this trial. Having your input would be invaluable to me."

Without hesitation, Gloria hugged Brad tightly and said, "You are the best!"

Opening arguments were Monday. Gloria wore her black worsted wool suit with a high collared silk blouse. She understated her jewelry, wearing the pearl and jade button earrings and matching pin that the Laras had given her for her college graduation gift. She was never without her gold watch, a gift from her parents for law school graduation. Jorge smiled when he saw it on her wrist. He had taken a personal day to see his daughter seek justice.

Gloria was the perfect drama queen, sparing the jury nothing. The gore of the broken beer bottle severing the victim's scrotum and nearly severing his penis was enough to make the judge squirm and several of the jurors to grimace. The defense argued that it was clearly a case of mistaken identity.

The accused, David Niles, sat stoically as the story unfolded. Gloria told the jurors that David was known for his comical impressions of gay men and often entertained his friends by dressing in drag. He once hosted a Halloween party as Dolly Parton. Fueled by alcohol, he allegedly attacked Will Baleaux, a known male prostitute who approached him in the parking lot on Wynkoop Street. Gloria chose her words carefully, saying that Niles lost all control with each punch and kick he foisted upon Will Baleaux.

"... he became more and more energized...fueled by his hatred of gays, getting into the rhythm of pounding the flesh and then picking up a broken beer bottle and finishing the job."

George Anderson, the defense attorney was a seasoned gray haired Perry Mason type. Brad knew him by reputation and was anxious to see him in action against Gloria. For Brad, it would be a learning experience and one that he would draw from in future trials. He was hooked after opening arguments. Anderson's depiction of an innocent David Niles was convincing. The soldier was fresh out of Afghanistan and newly enrolled at Metro State College, studying computer science. His life so far was without blemish. This sad situation was one of mistaken identity and Anderson would prove it beyond a shadow of a doubt. David Niles would walk out a free man and go on to live an exemplary life.

Gloria gained confidence as the trial progressed into the third day. Brad dropped in when he could and promised Gloria he would be in the courtroom when she called her star witness to the stand. True to his word, that Friday morning he took his seat in the last row, eager to see his new girl in action.

"Mr. Goodwyn, please state your full name," said Gloria.

"John Norman Goodwyn."

"Mr. Goodwyn, please tell us your street name and what you do for a living."

"I'm known as Johnny B Good To Me and I am an escort and personal assistant."

" In other words, Mr. Goodwyn, you are a male prostitute are you not?"

"Well, yeah, I guess so."

"Mr. Goodwyn, or do you mind if I call you Johnny?"

"No Ma'am, I prefer it."

"How do you know the victim, Will Baleaux?"

"We work together a lot...look out for each other."

"Does that mean that the two of you hustled customers for your services?"

"You could say that."

"Johnny, please explain in your own words what transpired the night of July 23rd, 2010."

Johnny proceeded to tell the hushed courtroom how he and Baleaux had been walking on Wynkoop Street at around midnight when Niles was trying to hail a cab. They approached Niles and asked if he was going to Cherry Creek and if they could share the cab. Lots of eye contact and smiles and Niles agreed but asked if they could show him some of the finer points of LODO before heading off to Cherry Creek.

Gloria approached the witness stand and asked, "Don't you really mean that the accused was flirting with you and his intent for a sexual encounter was evident?"

Anderson jumped up and loudly made his objection that Gloria was leading the witness. Gloria withdrew her comment but knew the jury would get her drift.

"Johnny, please continue to tell the court your recollection of what happened next."

Gloria had prepared Johnny to use clear language and not leave a lot to innuendo.

"Well, I knew his type. He too full of himself to say he wanted some butt. We see his kind a lot. No mistake there when he got hard and started takin Will's hand to his crotch."

Johnny told how he and Will Baleaux had serviced David Niles with a combo job, in the alley between Wynkoop and Blake Streets. Johnny explained the combo job to be oral and anal. Each was to receive $100 for the service.

"The dude was really into it. I mean he loved it. He be moaning real loud and we had to tell him to keep it down so nobody would hear. When he was done, we asked him to pay. Then he laughed and said he was a soldier and we owed him for what he done in Iraq. He threw down a twenty and said it was all he had."

Gloria asked, "Don't you guys get the money up front?"

"Most times, yeah," replied Goodwin. "But if the dude is looking rich, sometimes we get a lot more than what we might ask for, especially if we go combo. Money is real good for combo, a lot more than one doing and one watching...so, we wait if the guy looks rich."

Gloria prompted Johnny to continue.

"He walked over to the parking lot and got out his car keys. He hit the button and the lights went on. So Will and me, we ran after him. And Will, he got all upset and said he ain't no patriot and he no give no freebies to nobody. Then, the dude, he went crazy, threw Will down and started beatin' on him. I tried to help Will but soldier boy hit me over ma head with a beer bottle. I don't remember much else."

Gloria confirmed with Johnny that he woke up in the trauma center at Denver General Hospital.

"How long have you and Will Baleaux worked together in the Denver area?"

"About six months. We hitchhiked here from New York."

Brad took in every word and abruptly and discreetly left. He hoped Johnny didn't recognize him. It had been five years ago in Hell's Kitchen. Brad had gone slumming with the first years and wound up drinking till last call. He was put in a cab by the bartender. Johnny was walking the neighborhood. Brad told the cabbie to pull over and give the guy a ride. It was cold out and the poor guy might freeze. Brad only remembered waking up with Johnny in his bed. He gave him $1,000 and told him to never, ever contact him.

Gloria asked her witness if he could identify the man who had been serviced and who had beaten Johnny and mutilated Will. Johnny pointed to David Niles. Johnny also noticed a tall man in the middle of the last row, getting up to leave. He looked vaguely familiar.

Brad was sweating. He feared that Johnny might recognize him. Brad's practice was flourishing and he was in a good place, comfortable with himself and comfortable with a woman who was his equal in intellect and in ambition. He wished he could fall in love with her as she was the perfect compliment to him, and timing was right for taking a wife.

Johnny never forgot a big trick. If the money was good, then he knew he was truly Johnny B Good To Me. No one had ever given him $1,000 for an evening of sex. But, the guy in New York was desperate to be serviced, in every way that Johnny knew how. Johnny was spent and felt he deserved the $1,000, doled out in crisp $100 bills that the trick kept in a coffee can in his freezer.

No names were ever mentioned. But Johnny wasn't raised by idiots and grabbed a piece of junk mail when Brad was getting his hard cold cash out of the freezer. Johnny knew that Brad was ashamed of his proclivities and also knew that eventually, he would need another visit, and Johnny would like another $1,000. The junk mail was addressed to Bradley A. Stockman, Esq.

The face was a blur in the back of the courtroom. Johnny was nervous as the prosecutor questioned him. Recognition came when the prosecutor asked him how long he had been in Denver. Johnny noticed sudden movement in the back of the courtroom and thought he knew the tall man making his way from the middle of the row. It was the haircut, the elegant style and the clean-shaven pretty boy face. Could it be the dream trick? It was a while back and Johnny couldn't be sure. But the guy sure resembled the dream trick.

That night, Gloria called Brad and asked him what he thought of her day in court. Brad said he could only stay a short time and missed her star witness questioning. He was noticeably short and said he was working on a case and didn't have time to chat. He would try to come tomorrow or the next day. Again, his restlessness, his dissatisfaction and his anger at himself made him sick, literally. Brad opened up a bottle of wine, drank it down with cold pizza and threw up.

Gloria was baffled. Was this the same guy who volunteered to be her secret coach in a high profile trial that could boost her career? What was bothering him and what was so damn important in his workload that he couldn't even give her five minutes for a recap of the day?

Gloria had to talk herself out of self-doubt on the romance. She never looked better than when out with Brad. Date prep was a beautification project in front of her mirror, with every cosmetic trick used to be Brad worthy. Gloria even blew $1,500 on spiffy attire. He surely couldn't fault her for their legal conversations as it could rival anything on Law & Order. Gloria didn't have the luxury of time to worry about romance. She was kicking ass in the courtroom and needed a conviction.

Gloria next questioned the doctor at the trauma center and the urologist who would continue to treat the victim. Both doctors revealed that Will Baleaux had AIDS. The look on Niles face said it all. She rested her case late afternoon on Wednesday.

The defense attorney had his work cut out for him as Gloria had done an excellent job. But George Anderson was no slouch in the courtroom. He had age and experience and a winning streak for tough cases. But the evidence was overwhelming. Fingerprints on the broken beer bottle at the scene matched those of David Niles.

Members of the jury were noticeably upset when Gloria brought Will Baleaux to the witness stand. His positive identification of David Niles and his sobbing surely swayed the doubters.

Gloria called Brad the night before her closing argument. He let it go to voice mail. She had no clue as to what went wrong with the friendship let alone the romance. But, she had a trial to win and couldn't give in to her disappointment. Gloria's close was short, inclusive of the severity of the crime and the preponderance of evidence proving without a shadow of doubt that it was David Niles who victimized both Will Baleaux and Johnny Goodwyn. And with the stunning news of the victim's

HIV status, Niles all but confessed with his facial expression and body language.

David Niles was convicted of assault with intent to kill. The jury was unanimous in their guilty verdict. Jorge and Elizabeth were never so proud of their daughter. She had indeed exceeded their wildest expectations. Gloria was on the front page of the Denver Post and the cover story of the Denver Business Journal. Her future was looking mighty good.

Gloria went to visit Will Baleaux when he was in hospice care. Johnny Goodwyn was also there. Will was too far gone for the magic pills and treatments to extend his life. The doctors asked him to try and recall his sexual partners so that they could be tested. There were so many. Johnny was tested and he was HIV positive. Working together and being reckless will do that. Johnny asked Gloria if she knew the lawyer named Stockman who had a full page ad in the Yellow Pages. She nodded yes.

Screaming Purple Jesus

In Vino Veritas is a well-known phrase that translates to "in wine there is truth." Often, the truth or something close to it comes out with the drinking of beer, gin, vodka, whiskey and just about any kind of firewater.

How many husbands and wives have had the morning after regret for unloading their deepest and darkest of thoughts while under the influence? Loose-lipped liquor talk has been responsible for some of the most infamous marital fights and has for centuries, altered the plans of the betrothed.

Who could forget Martha and George going at it on stage while the audience cringed with recognition? Whoever said, "sticks and stones can break my bones but words can never hurt me" must have been a robot that never had a meaningful relationship. What you are about to read will hopefully serve as a reminder that the less said is the best said, especially when drinking a Screaming Purple Jesus on the rocks.

One particularly icy day in mid December, I decided to take the bus downtown to do some Christmas shopping. No sense driving on the ice when the bus stopped right outside my condo complex in suburban Minneapolis.

I put on my fashionable red rubber cowboy boots and my favorite long coat, purchased while on a ski trip in Vail, Colorado. It was black boiled wool with wonderful hand embroidery on both the front and back. I wore my cashmere black turtleneck sweater and favorite black jeans. I put a new battery in my Rudolph pin and fastened it to my right lapel. Rudolph was a treasure from a Christmas past who always brought a smile and an occasional comment from those who still believed in the favorite reindeer. I was quite pleased with my appearance and it put me in a festive mood. Going shopping and looking good will do that.

I didn't mind taking the bus if I got on after rush hour when it was less crowded with the coughers and sneezers. Plus, I could blow the money on gifts that I saved on gas and all day parking. I had only a short wait for the 10:18 bus going to the Nicollete Mall. I sat up front near the heater and quite enjoyed gazing out at the fresh white snow that had fallen the night before.

My agenda that day was to find the gifts for the out of town relatives. Small things for my cousins and elderly aunt that could be put in a shoe box, such as a good book or other small but practical gifts that wouldn't cost an arm and a leg to ship. I had my list of movies and was on the lookout for deals on the Christmas music. My elderly Aunt Shirley was a religious fanatic who would appreciate the Midnight Mass numbers that Susan Boyle sang. I had a winter scene plastic shopping bag from the dollar store and when it was filled, I would treat myself to a facial at Skyway Spa.

I took off my gloves and reached inside my purse for the crossword that I had ripped out of the morning newspaper. I filled in the easy ones and had to think about the more challenging clues on sports and classical music. A few stops later, a heavy set woman got on, greeting the bus driver cheerfully with a loud, "Merry-Merry to you my friend and drive carefully! It's a skating rink out there."

The bus driver laughed and said he had no choice but to do that as the snow plows had made it a collision course with the piles of wet snow removed from the main roads. The animated and friendly passenger noticed Rudolph blinking and thus began one of the most memorable of my conversations with complete strangers.

"Lordy, look at that nose! Where'd you ever find that?"

I told her that it was a Secret Santa gift from my working days as a substitute teacher. Rudolph was the gift that kept on giving year after year. I pulled him out of my box of Christmas decorations every year and wore him proudly on my favorite coat. The inquisitive passenger was African American. I was in a friendly mood and I asked her where she was from and if she had voted for Obama.

"Born and raised in Alabama and hell yes, I voted for Obama," she said. "I voted early and then volunteered all day at my precinct."

I had found a political ally and I introduced myself.

"I'm Wilma Drysdale and I'm a die-hard Democrat from Detroit originally." She high fived me and said, "Gertude Johnson and I'm pleased to know you."

We both trashed the Republicans and discussed the things we wanted Obama to fix. Gertrude was high on education and hoped that Obama would improve the public schools, beef up the lunch programs and make it easier for single parents to get help with childcare.

I asked her to tell me about herself. Married? Kids? Gertrude was animated, speaking with her hands as well as her melodious voice. Her laugh and smile were infectious and I quite liked everything she had to say.

"Honey, I got kids and grand kids who got kids," she said. "Moved here for my husband's work. He died a few years back and I'm retired from cooking at the Presbyterian Home."

I told Gertrude that I divorced the attorney from hell who took my money for law school and then took up with his secretary. I added that I was still on the hunt for Mr. Right, and that this time around, I would steer clear of lawyers.

"Mmmm mmmm mmmm! Amen to that," said Gertrude, loud enough for the entire bus to hear. Then she added, "Girl, I hate lawyers and even if Obama's married to one, I still hate em."

I asked why. She got considerably louder and said, "They a bunch a nasties and tried to turn my man against me, that's why!"

Now, I was hooked and as the bus was at least another twenty minutes to the entrance to the Nicollete Mall, I got into it. "Did your husband try to divorce you?"

"Hell no, baby. The goddamn lawyers tried to put me in prison."

The entire bus went silent. The bus driver was ever so grateful that we were sitting up front so he wouldn't have to strain to get the rest of the story. I forgot all manners and appropriate public conversation. Couldn't help myself as this was as good as anything I would ever hear riding a bus downtown.

"What did you do to your husband," I asked, eager for the salacious details.

"I shot him," said Gertrude as calmly as if she said she kissed him. I still couldn't help myself. I remembered her saying earlier that her husband had died a few years ago.

"Jesus Christ woman! Did you kill him?"

"Oh no baby, I didn't kill him. I jes' learnt him a lesson so's he not foget who he was married to."

By this time, the bus had picked up several more passengers. Those in the first four rows were captivated. Those in the back moved closer to hear.

"What did he do to forget that he was married to you," I asked.

"Got hisself confused and called home instead of a tramp's cell and called me the wrong name. Called me Debra, the second cousin of his brother in-law. Then he started saying shit like, I got some grape juice and you got the hooch so we can have some Purple Jesus to get you in da mood."

I remembered vomiting Screaming Purple Jesus and cringed with the thought of the grape juice and gin coming back up after the Senior Prom. I never drank Welsh's again or used grape jelly on my peanut butter sandwiches. All I could say, was, "Oh my God, tell me the rest of it!"

"Well, my husband's name was Leroy and we called him Lucky Leroy. I tell him over and over that he was lucky to be married to me as I was a good cook and good at other things, if ya know what I mean. So, Lucky ain't got no reason to go drink Purple Jesus with a tramp. He called me Debra and I knew where Debra lived."

"Back up," I said. "What did you say when you answered and he called you the wrong name?"

"I never said nothin....just hung up the phone."

I asked with shameful excitement, "Did you go over to Debra's?"

"Yes Ma'am! I took my lady piece with me and went through the back door. That fool Debra never fixed the broke lock. She was pretty but she was trash. I walked into her bedroom and shot Lucky where he like to feel it."

I feared the worst and wondered if she had shot his jewels off.

"Ah know what you thinking and I ain't that stupid. Got him in the leg and he be bleedin real good. Debra screamed and called the Po-lice. They sent an ambulance and Lucky be cryin' and beggin' me to forgive him. Cops tried to arrest me but when Lucky done with the Emergency Room and he be in the hospital bed, he say he won't be pressin' no charges. He knew what he done and he still loved me."

I backed up to the comment about Gertrude hating lawyers.

"Where do the lawyers come into the story?"

"Them cops said that Debra's bedroom was a crime scene. One of em' told her to go after me for breakin into her back door. But it wasn't locked. I just came a callin and looky who I found in bed with her! Fool Debra calls one of them TV lawyers and tried to get me for breakin' and enterin' and assault. But it weren't her that got shot. It be Lucky. Cost me and Lucky our trip money to fight it."

So, now I had to know how things worked out between Gertrude and Lucky.

"Did you forgive Lucky?"

"Oh yes and Lucky got Lucky again. But I told him that if he gonna stomp on my love, he best be takin' his shoes off or he not be so Lucky next time. He never drank Purple Jesus again!"

Gertrude said that she missed Lucky but stayed busy with her big family. She got off at Hennepin and I rode the next few blocks to Nicollete.

Designated Driver

She had an unlikely nickname for a sometime and somewhat illegal taxi driver. They called her Aunt Dee Dee, short for designated driver. Agnes Marie Kramer drove the drunk, the stoned, the naughty and the criminal. No questions asked, just a thousand in cash for anything up to 50 miles. She drove an old Suburban and dressed in black. If need be she would provide breakfast, snacks, bloody Mary's and comfort to her patrons as required.

Agnes was an emergency room nurse, retired and bored. She got her nickname one night while helping to celebrate the birthday of one of her former co-workers. Not one for over indulging in anything, Agnes volunteered to be the designated driver if anyone needed her. She re-invented herself that fateful night and began a very lucrative business, working sporadically and most often at night.

The evening started off at Betty's house and progressed to the Roma Café, where a private room had been reserved. The happy hour began at 5 o'clock. Betty served *sauvignon blanc* and caviar. The group had worked in the same hospital for decades. They had seen it all together, the births, the deaths and the bizarre. It was best not to get any of them started on the ER stories of Halloween night or full moon crazies.

They were a family of medical folks, working hard and eager to play hard when they could. Senior most among them was Dr. George Frazier, a pathologist, then Dr. Bob Lewis, an ophthalmologist. George and Bob were sixty plus. The younger kids, late forties to fifty something were nurse Alice Larson from the intensive care unit, thoracic surgeon Dr. Ken Harvey, oncologist Dr. Jill Abrams and Frankie Morgan, the head of the hospital foundation.

March 30th was Ken Harvey's 58th birthday. His wife was in Europe with her sister, touring Cathedrals and buying shoes and trinkets she didn't need. His two sons were living out of state and he had no one to celebrate with. Bob called Betty and she organized a fun evening of eating and drinking.

"Hey, I just bought a case of this," said Betty." It was the wine of the month at my wine club and it's really quite good."

"Fancy shmancy with the silver wine goblets," said Frankie. "Is it supposed to make the wine taste better?"

'You be the judge, and have some caviar to enhance your taste buds!"

It was so good to be out of the hospital and away from the stress of dealing with patients and insurance companies. This was their first get together in several months. They needed a mood enhancement. George had a wicked sense of humor, born out of necessity, as he had to lighten up the darkness of the morgue where most of his work was done. He loudly gave the command that they should celebrate life, and bring the gang out of their doldrums.

Ken was a bit down of late, sad over his wife's wanderlust and feeling the need for excitement. Bob was gay and had lost his life partner to pancreatic cancer. Jill was four years into a legal separation from a doofus inventor still trying to sell his patent on a solar powered motorbike. Betty was a widow of ten years and an excellent but bossy surgical nurse. Agnes divorced her husband when he got caught embezzling. Alice was an unclaimed treasure with a few failed romances and an excellent facelift that belied her years. She ran five miles every other day, played tennis and could pass for 40.

"This is yummy and so salty," said Alice as she heaped a man size portion of black caviar on a toast point.

"Did you run today?" asked Jill.

"Yeah, and I did an extra mile as I knew I'd over eat and have a few drinks."

"Well, you are replenishing your salt with all that caviar."

Alice washed it down with a full goblet of wine. It complimented the fish taste and went down easy as it was perfectly chilled. Betty prided herself on entertaining with style. She put the bottles of wine in the freezer just before her guests arrived. The black mountain of caviar was served on a cut glass serving plate, garnished with parsley. The toast points were laid out in a pattern that spelled out *Ken is 58!!!* Helium filled birthday balloons floated around the living room. It was going to be a fun night for Ken and his pals.

Betty knew Ken loved country music. He played it on the boom box during long surgeries. Betty had her mix of Johnny Cash, Wynona, and Willy Nelson playing on the Bose system she bought herself last Christmas.

Betty was Ken's favorite scrub nurse. She could anticipate his needs and keep the team on their toes. Betty had wanted to go to medical school but life got in the way. She loved the operating room and the thrill of saving lives. Betty also loved Ken but kept her feelings to herself. She was happiest when working and always the professional. Patients loved her, as she was their fearless advocate, often waging war with hospital staff to keep her post ops happy and on the road to recovery.

Agnes had a half goblet of wine. She added water and ice to make it last. She was a drinking snob who never lost control. Agnes thoroughly enjoyed watching others make idiots of themselves. It gave her one up on them and she liked being the rescuer. She also delighted in never letting any of them forget that gratitude was a real bitch.

"I appoint myself designated driver for you wild and crazy party people."

"You hear that gang?" asked George. "We can cut loose."

Agnes had done this in the past, taking car keys from her friends, driving them home or putting them into cabs. She suggested that everyone leave their cars at Betty's and pile into her Chevy Suburban.

Roma Café was a gourmet's dream for authentic Italian food. They had a family style assortment of pasta, fish and chicken, plenty of Chianti and Galliano with the birthday cheesecake dessert.

"Ken dear," said Betty. "We have a surprise for your birthday gift."

"What might that be?" he asked.

"We are all taking a dance lesson at Cowboy Joe's. There's a band tonight and they have a singer that sounds more like Kenny Chesney than Kenny Chesney."

George and Bob split the dinner bill and they all piled into the Suburban. Agnes had never been to Cowboy Joe's but Betty knew the way. She had been taking lessons for the past month. The country two-step was her favorite. Tonight's lesson was the line dance, very appropriate for the mate-less friends. No touchy feely stuff and innocent enough for all to enjoy.

Alice popped for the first round of beers. The raucous voice of Hank Williams Junior got them on the dance floor. The dance instructor was as hilarious as she was gorgeous. A full six feet tall in her sequined red boots, Sagebrush Sally demonstrated the steps with hip action and shoulder dips. Watching Ken watch her was worth the price of the lessons and then some. Ken was a mess of feet and ridiculous hand gestures. He didn't seem to notice or care as he gulped from his long neck and drooled over Sally. Betty sashayed her way over so she could dance next to him. He didn't notice. Betty became annoyed.

Bob and Alice got the steps easily. They cracked each other up with their lively singing along to the music. Agnes struggled but got better as she positioned herself right behind Alice and followed her moves.

Jill never made it to the lesson dance floor as a mustached hunk of man asked her to dance the country waltz on the main floor. They danced well together. Jill had lost all inhibitions back at Roma and was now flirting like a teenager.

"You are such a good dancer! Have you done this a lot?"

"Learned back in Texas," he said.

The hunk said little, but then, he didn't have to. The broad shoulders, long legs, black eyes peering out of a Stetson and confident hand on Jill's waist spoke all the conversation she wanted. Jill was sort of single, buzzed and horny as hell. The hunk felt the heat and moved Jill in a little closer as they danced to *Amarillo By Morning*. Jill knew the words, singing softly in his ear as they did the country cheek to cheek. Bad cowboy, come to Mama!

Frankie did his best to learn the routine with Sagebrush Sally as she demonstrated with exaggerated moves. Between dance instructions, Sally accompanied Carrie Underwood on the sound system belting out *Cowboy Casanova*. Frankie picked up the steps, laughing at himself and was having fun. He deserved a laugh or two since he had his last fling with an ex nun who left him for another nun.

Betty couldn't stand Ken's ogling Sally. What was she, this Sagebrush Sally Slut? Maybe 30? Probably couldn't read beyond the 8th grade level and wouldn't know her way around a library or a kitchen. But damn, she had that body and long dark curls and not a wrinkle or sag in sight. Betty was jealous and needed to get Ken off the dance floor. She bought the gang a round of tequila shots and challenged them to a game of pool in the back room of Cowboy Joe's.

Ken didn't want to leave the dance floor but lucky for Betty, Ken tripped over the klutz next to him. His back went out and he let out a groan and doubled over. Betty helped him stand up, took his arm and led him off.

The poolroom was where the action was for the competitive. Graduates of the dance floor took up their sticks, chalked them and made their bets, tossing tens and twenties into a weathered straw hat. It was less dangerous than riding the motorized bull, or was it?

George and Bob each had pool tables in their homes. Bob's was an antique mahogany table from the early 1900's, a gift from his late partner. George got his off e-Bay. Bob was about as good as Minnesota Fats and George could more than hold his own. Frankie played occasionally at the pub down the street from the hospital. Alice looked terrific bending and stretching for a shot but couldn't do much but entertain the on lookers. Agnes sat out, drank her club soda and placed a twenty on Bob. Betty told Ken he needed more tequila to dull the pain. She ordered double shots.

The poolroom regulars were anxious to take some bills from the new players. George was at table one, Bob at table two and Frankie and Alice at table three. George tossed two tens in the hat and played a decent game but lost to the guy with tattoos wearing a rodeo prize belt buckle. Bob played miserably and lost his twenty to the guy who looked like John Wayne's twin.

His name was Lane Hauser. He drove a truck in the winter and did the rodeo circuit in the summer.

Agnes berated Bob for losing her money. Frankie and Alice were shit-faced, laughing and couldn't care less who won or lost.

"Avenge yourself man," said Hauser. "Increase the pot and play to win."

Bob threw in two fifties. Agnes tossed another twenty in. George came over, as did Frankie and Alice. They each tossed two twenties in. Tattoo guy rounded up a few of his pals and they tossed in an assortment of bills, including a few C notes. Easy money from the mild looking skinny player who had downed his Jose Quervo shot and was sucking on his beer. He was most certainly impaired and would lose again to Lane.

Bob won the break toss and proceeded to sink every ball, calling his last shot while maintaining his blank expressionless face. Frankie grinned while Alice shrieked with delight. George just sat there. Bob asked Agnes to collect the winnings and he foolishly asked Lane if he wanted to avenge himself.

Mistake! Lane Hauser didn't like to lose. He didn't even get a shot! His buddies were loud and raucous with their reactions and weren't at all impressed with the pip-squeak who hustled Lane.

"What the fuck? I see we got ourselves a goddamn hustler here," said tattoo guy.

Frankie shot his mouth off and told the cowboys not to be sore losers. Big mistake.

Agnes caught the signs, shoved the cash into her shoulder bag and whispered to George that she was going to get the car and meet everyone at the back door.

"Who you calling a sore loser ass hole," asked Lane.

"You, of course," replied Frankie.

Bigger mistake. Lane had a reputation to defend so he picked Frankie up by the collar and tossed him into the side of the pool table. Frankie grabbed a long neck as he was going down and threw it at Lane. He missed and hit the tattoo guy, who let out a grunt and called Frankie a dickhead. Frankie reverted to his youth and yelled back,

"...proud to be one, you girly pussy!" Now we're talking! Testosterone Shower!

Bob grabbed his stick and assumed his fighting stance. Did I mention that Bob was the sensei at the dojo and that George was his assistant?

George grabbed a stick and the two karate kids took on the sore losers. Fists and anger collided with skill and speed. A roundhouse kick to Hauser's ribs followed by a stick to his shins incapacitated the dude. Score one for Bob.

George took out tattoo guy. A blast across his back knocked the wind out of him. George was quick to notice another brute coming out of nowhere swinging a chair. George ducked, grabbed the brute's other arm and twisted it out of its socket. Bob blocked a punch from a guy from table three and landed a chop in his solar plexus. Then, Bob did what all stand up brawlers do in a situation like this and asked, "You like it, you love it, now, you want some more of it?"

This thrilled Alice to pieces. This was too much fun. She cheered her boys on. "Go Bobby Baby! Go Georgie boy!"

Huge mistake. Frankie thought this might get problematic so he grabbed Alice and headed for the main floor where they took refuge among the dancers.

"Are you stupid? What the hell are you egging them on for," asked Frankie. "We gotta get the fuck out of here, and Alice, for Christ's sake, keep your goddamn mouth shut."

About that time, while the band played *Red Neck Woman*, the bouncers rushed in to the poolroom. Two cowboys were writhing on the beer soaked floor, one of them retching as he had taken a hit in the belly from George. Out of socket guy could do nothing more than take shallow breaths between cursing.

George told the bouncers that this was a terrible situation and that he and Bob were each doctors and could help with the injured if needed. Betty knew she had to intervene so she let out a scream, "I'm bleedin' real bad!"

"We got this man, go help that lady over there."

Betty faked her injuries and let George and Bob assist her out the side door. She told Ken to get Frankie and Alice and to meet up with Agnes at the back door. Jill was nowhere to be found.

Ken's back wasn't as painful as it was an hour ago. Plenty of drinks and adrenalin, plus he was distracted by the fight. He walked out to the main dance floor and looked for Frankie and Alice. He spotted them and gave them the over here signal. The three scouted the room for Jill. Ken told Frankie, "Agnes can come back for her. We gotta move now!"

Agnes was waiting for them, double-parked by the back door service entrance. The security guard had protested but softened up when she explained that she was the designated driver and had a mission to accomplish. She winked at him and slipped him a ten.

"Now, remember to buckle up, shut up and don't throw up." Agnes loved being in charge.

Betty locked arms with Ken in the third seat. George and Bob were in the middle seat and crouched down so no one would see them. Frankie sat between them. Alice rode up front with Agnes. Alice was on a roll, belting out *Me and Bobby Magee*. Good choice for a sing along as it was sleeting and the windshield wipers were indeed keeping time.

Agnes grabbed her chance to lecture the naughty and let loose with, "How old is this group? You're all a bunch of juvenile delinquents and you'd all be in county lock up if not for me, your kind and dedicated designated driver."

Bob cracked up and told her she had an enormous cue stick up her ass. Frankie commented that Bob wished he had a stick up his ass. George chimed in with, "Well fuck us, Aunt Dee Dee, designated driver! We ain't had this much fun since we won the wheel chair race on New Year's Eve!"

Frankie asked, "So, Ken, how's your birthday party so far?"

"Best ever," he said.

"Where the hell is Jill?" asked Agnes.

"Probably getting laid," answered Frankie.

Frankie had seen Jill waltzing around with the Mustache and figured the relationship had matured over the evening. Ken grinned and said, "Getting laid! God, that sounds good!"

"Doesn't it though," whispered Betty in his ear.

Agnes drove the gang back to Betty's. There was no way she would let any of them drive their own cars back to their homes. She got very officious and demanded keys from each. Betty had already pocketed Ken's. Agnes turned the TV on and found a good movie on HBO. Frankie retrieved the remaining bottles of *sauvignon blanc*. Sometime between the first hour of the movie, they were all asleep, sprawled on the sectional sofa. All except Ken and Betty.

Ever the professional, Betty told Ken that he needed to lie down on a heating pad to lesson the severity of his spinal ouchy. She led him to her bedroom, locking the door behind her. One thing led to another and soon Betty was riding her cowboy and he forgot all about his aching back. Yeah, it was the best birthday ever for Ken.

While they were each enjoying the afterglow, he confessed that his wife was no fun. Betty replied that that was tragic. Ken complained that he had been the provider of a grand house, a BMW, a country club membership, educations for their sons and supported her dim witted sister. All he ever wanted from her was a decent blowjob. He was desperate for one but she refused, calling him a perverted pig. Betty said it was downright mean for her to treat him this way. A damn shame. He deserved better and then Betty granted his wish.

Agnes eventually drove back to Cowboy Joe's to find Jill. She had the good sense to park in the lot far away from the ambulance at the side door. It was 1 am and the crowd was festive. Where could Jill be?

Agnes went inside and looked around. She recognized one of the servers and approached her. "I'm looking for a friend from our group. Do you remember her? Bleached blonde, pretty and was dancing with a tall guy with a mustache."

"Lots of mustaches in here tonight, but somebody blonde just left with Scott Henderson."

"So, who is Scott and how do I find him?"

"He owns the place and is probably in his office with the door locked."

Well, wasn't this a prickly pear to contend with! Agnes was directed to the office on the second floor. She loudly knocked on the door. "Jill honey, its Aunt Dee Dee here to take you home."

Jill was making sounds that Agnes recognized. She thought it best to write Jill a note and slip it under the door. Agnes wrote, "Call Aunt Dee Dee Designated Driver For A Safe Ride Home." Who knew how long it might take? Agnes drove home and made herself a cup of peppermint tea. She dozed off in front of the TV and had four hours of sleep before the phone started ringing. The call was from Jill. "Agnes! Can you come and get me?"

Eager to punish Jill for her frolic, Agnes feigned grogginess and replied, "Jill dear, I tried to collect you several hours ago but it seemed you were quite busy with the upper management of the saloon."

"Agnes, I'll pay you a thousand bucks to get over here and get me, now!"

"So, what's the emergency?"

"His wife! Please Agnes, hurry."

"Aunt Dee Dee is on her way."

Jill was waiting at the corner, a half block away from Cowboy Joe's. Agnes pulled up and Jill got in, telling Agnes to punch it. Mrs. Mustache was on her way to collect Mustache who was passed out on the couch. Mrs. Mustache had left a threatening voice mail, describing what she was going to do to her husband who couldn't keep it in his pants, and his rhinestone whore who was a tramp home-wreaker. Agnes thought better than to lecture Jill and simply smiled, thinking how great it was that she had averted a double homicide.

Agnes pulled up to Betty's driveway where Jill had parked her Prius. She luckily had been the last to arrive at Betty's happy hour and wasn't blocked by the other vehicles. "Want to come in for coffee and some breakfast with the gang," asked Agnes.

"No! Please Agnes, not a word of this!" Jill drove off, leaving Agnes to wonder if she would keep her word on the thousand dollars.

It was now 5 in the morning and hangovers were on the horizon for her friends. Agnes drove over to Wal-Mart and picked up coffee, English muffins, bananas, peanut butter and Bloody Mary mix. She was sure Betty had plenty of vodka.

Agnes walked into Betty's with the groceries. The TV was still on and the drunks were still sleeping it off. She made coffee, set up the provisions and waited for the first to awaken. She left the TV on, changing the channel to CNN.

While Agnes was sipping her second cup, Alice woke up. She was still a little giggly from her wonderful evening and playfully awakened her friends with a little singing. She was on her second chorus of *You Are My Sunshine* when Frankie said he needed to be sick and asked where the bathroom was. George and Bob were next to awaken and head straight for the coffee. Agnes poured them each a mug. Bob asked, "Hey, where's Ken? Where's Jill?"

Agnes said Ken was last seen with Betty. He was in pain and Betty was tending to his needs in her bedroom. George grinned at Bob who did the thumbs up. Agnes told them that Jill had been found at Cowboy Joe's and was safely home. No other explanations from Agnes. Silence and more coffee. George said what they were all thinking. "Great birthday party, amnesia and all."

Agnes got lovely thank you notes from each of her passengers. Jill kept her word and enclosed her check for a thousand dollars. Scott Henderson woke up before his wife got there. He used Agnes' note to explain that he had hired a designated driver service and was unusually busy that night. Agnes came out of retirement, became a night owl and was paid in cash for her weekend work.

Low Tide Walkers

Dr. Gerald Zimmerman was a pragmatic psychiatrist in San Diego. He was the shrink who told his patients that hurt people, hurt people. He got right to the point, often interrupting a patient's plea for pity.

"Let me stop you right there," he said. "You are not in this alone. Everyone who knows that the sun comes up in the morning and goes down in the evening, also knows that to be alive is to get hurt sometimes."

Doc Z, as he was known by his patients, specialized in alcohol and substance abuse. He saw the drinkers, the junkies and their families. He told every drinker and junkie that the cunning illness of addiction was as greedy as the most contagious disease. It sucked family, friends and colleagues into its vortex. There was no immunity from its ravages of the mind and body. If there were a vaccine to prevent addiction, Doc Z would be a billionaire. But there wasn't and Doc Z wasn't motivated by big bucks.

Without exception, all his patients were angry with themselves but powerless to stop using. Doc Z did his best to give each of his patients the weapons to fight the demons of addiction. "No self-scolding allowed! Feeling sorry for yourself is the worst kind of indoor sport. I'm going to help you get a new daily plan. Like a newborn baby on a schedule of eating every four hours, you will soothe yourself and others throughout everyday of the rest of your life, starting right now. You are here and asking for help. This the best gift to yourself and your family."

Doc Z made great analogies that his patients could relate to. He told them that carrying a heavy load of hurt was like having a pet piranha in your underwear. "Your own hurt will get you in the shorts if you let it. Unresolved hurt and addiction go hand in hand. Toxic pain is the piranha that devours its prey, so pray you never let a piranha get too close."

Doc Z could have been wealthy but he wasn't in it for the money. He wasn't into psychoanalyses and mumbo jumbo. He was a fixer. Doc found people and their problems endlessly interesting and often said that going to work everyday was exciting. Doc never knew what he might learn about human behavior and the strength of the human spirit.

Doc saw patients in the hospital and in his modest office. He was also a volunteer at the San Diego County Jail and once a month, drove to the Lompoc Federal Prison to conduct what he called bad ass group sessions. Doc outed the illiterate at Lompoc, where the majority of inmates had debilitating learning disabilities that prevented them from benefiting even a primary school education.

The R's Gang was started by Doc and the chaplains. The R's Gang learned reading, writing and arithmetic in a safe and humiliation free classroom. Retired teachers and off duty military from nearby Vandenberg Air Force Base came for visitation and led tutoring. Doc hit the thrift shops every Saturday, buying books to bring to the jail and to the penitentiary. He found that the inmates loved good stories of adventure, of triumph over adversity and all kinds of wild life and nature photo books. His late wife Beth had left over 500 issues of National Geographic neatly boxed in their garage. Doc found a good home for them and the over 300 books on tape that Beth enjoyed when she was sick.

Every patient, no matter where they met Doc got the same pep talk. "Life is what you make of it and you wouldn't be here if you were making the best of yours, so work with me and let's get healthy. There is no dilly-dallying here and no whining about the unfairness of life. Life isn't fair and I have yet to meet anyone not from a dysfunctional family. If you're not willing to do some work, take meds if necessary and participate in group sessions, then don't waste your time or mine. I don't need your money and I don't need another pain in my ass. Anyone can be born to crazy parents or encounter crazy people and anyone can be born with a chemical imbalance. So let's figure it out."

Group therapy sessions followed three months of individual sessions. Group members made up a psychological museum of victims and perpetrators where tears were shed, tempers flared, shame and fear were exposed. Nobody made it out sweat free.

But, then, Doc died and the museum got lonely. Group members commiserated at Doc's memorial service. They decided to meet every week for a walk on the beach at low tide. The organizers emailed the time and location, delegated the topic for discussion and assigned the snacks, coffee and soft drinks.

The first walk was at 7 in the morning at Imperial Beach a week after Doc's memorial service. It was organized by Hank Shemanski.

Hank was a perpetrator. He spent most of his life as a misanthrope. His was a slow burn at first, like a Bunsen Burner that never got turned off. This was a dangerous heat. Hank's temper flared up without warning, a lightening bolt hitting dead wood, quick to ignite, taking down whatever and whomever was nearby. It was a problem and Hank knew it. He chose to ignore it.

During his senior year at Tufts, one of his college fraternity brothers gifted him a stack of personalized cards that read:

Hank Shemanski
Is Truly Sorry For His Bad Behavior.
*On*_____

All Hank had to do was fill in the date and sign the card "Mea Culpa!"

Hank was academically brilliant but lacked impulse control. He was an over achiever at Tufts but failed in learning life lessons. Charming and very good looking, Hank could easily switch from charismatic eye candy to the creep with Manson eyes. Dr. Phil could do an entire season of shows on him. Hank's victims, as well as his family and friends, hadn't a clue as to how to handle him.

Hank was a strong type A personality with a short fuse. He hated incompetence and imperfection. He never gave himself the time to figure out why. Working was an escape and a legitimate one at that. He competed with everyone in everything. His fiercest competitor was himself. He stopped playing golf as it was too slow and he embarrassed himself with his angry frustration when he couldn't putt worth a damn. Instead, he got his game on at the downtown YMCA playing squash. He used all that pent up hate smacking the little black ball into the walls. Few could beat him.

This manic drive gained him several million dollars worth of cars, airplanes, houses and collectibles, such as first editions, sculptures and oil paintings. The ladies liked Hank a lot at first, and, why not? He was handsome, fun and generous with his money. But the nice Hank never lasted too long. The other Hank would emerge after a few months and then the poor girl got blasted with his criticism, jealousy, control and rage.

Some thought that Hank really disliked women. He treated them badly, as if they were chattel. Hank drank on the weekends. Some weekends, he drank a lot.

By the age of 43, Hank was an investment banker who made big bucks for his clients and for himself. That all changed when the investments in an oil and gas exploration venture went south. He lost millions for his clients and millions for himself. His marriage was a mess. Hank's young wife was at her wits end trying to deal with his anger and depression, completely at a loss as to how to fix it. She tried to be the perfect wife but there was no pleasing Hank. He blamed just about everything on her. Hank told her that she was stupid and beneath him intellectually, homely and too fair skinned, and unable to satisfy him. He told her he would rather jerk off than touch her, as she was not what he wanted. Hank also repeatedly told his wife that his mother had warned him not to marry her and that she had written to the Archdiocese of San Diego paving the way for a papal annulment, just in case Hank needed one.

Carol Shemanski was seven months pregnant with their second child when Hank totally lost it one night. He had been in a foul mood for months and started drinking heavily at a firm picnic. Carol didn't want to attend as she was not feeling well and was uncomfortable watching Hank play football with the secretaries while she was big with child and busy watching their 19-month-old son. Hank called her a jealous bitch and told her to get into the Porsche and not embarrass him. She could watch the game with the other wives. She refused and said the entire firm knew Hank's secretary was mad for him and it was uncomfortable to watch, especially while she was pregnant and not feeling at all attractive.

Hank stormed off, calling her the C word and returned home late that night. He was drunk and combative. Drinking fueled his anger. Hank threw a shoe at his wife, hitting her smack in the face. She was startled and furious at him. She asked him, "Mama's boy feel like a real man now that you've hit your pregnant wife?"

Wrong thing to say to a guy with Mom issues. Those words were the gas on his bonfire. Hank went berserk. He picked his wife up and threw her into the wall, then picked her up and slammed her head into the solid oak door of their bedroom. He hit her on her neck, her shoulders and back, careful to avoid any direct hits to her face, as that would leave bruises. Carol screamed and told Hank to stop. Their toddler screamed, confused and terrified.

Hank was wild with hate, smelled of sweat and beer and couldn't stop, as it was so intoxicating to smack and pound this woman in his life. Carol grabbed their son and ran out the door to a neighbor's. Hank was ordered by the court to get psychiatric help. He only went for a few weeks. Carol gave him an ultimatum, continue getting help or she would divorce him. He didn't and she did. Carol got full custody of their son and newborn daughter, moved to upstate New York and never looked back.

Hank went on with his life, made millions again and only sought treatment when his son came to visit him one day. Hank's son asked him what bothered him so much that he was perpetually pissed. Hank was 58, worn down by the blend of shame and pride. He knew Doc Z from the YMCA and had beaten him in the last squash tournament. Doc Z was a nice guy and a hell of a good squash player. Hank swallowed his pride, made the appointment and began a psychiatric evaluation. He was diagnosed with bipolar disease brought on by severe childhood trauma. Hank participated in Doc Z's group therapy sessions that included abusers and their victims, twice a week for a year. Doc told Hank that every abuser is also a victim. "Who the hell wants to be either?" Doc asked.

The second walk was organized by Stella Cunningham. It took place at Coronado Beach, two weeks after Hank's walk.

Stella was a victim of the Second World War even though she wasn't born till 1950. Stella suffered her father's battle fatigue or as we now refer to it as post-traumatic stress disorder. Stella carried the heavy burden of being an adult child of an alcoholic till the weight brought down every meaningful relationship in her life.

Stella saw Doc Z on the local news one night discussing the effect that post-traumatic stress disorder has on the families of soldiers returning from Afghanistan. He added that this wasn't a new problem. Soldiers from every war were affected. He spoke about the rise of alcoholism in the years following 1945.

"Coping with a few drinks and cigarettes became the norm," said Doc Z. "Nobody wanted to talk about the atrocities of Europe or the Pacific. These heroic soldiers bottled it up and then hit the bottle big time. Now we use the phrase 'dysfunctional family dynamics.' For the children of those with post-traumatic stress disorder, there is hardly anything functional in the family. Most children of severe trauma victims have many of the same issues that adult children of alcoholics have."

Stella burst out crying. She knew just what Doc Z was talking about. Her own father had gone through hell fighting the Japanese. After her mother's funeral, Stella found three boxes of letters written to her mother from 1942 to 1945. Her father wrote every week. He told of his love and how he missed his beautiful sweetheart. Then he told of how better men than he were losing their minds, and he would lose his if this damn war didn't end soon. Stella's mother saved them all. Several had photos of the six months spent in Hawaii shortly after Pearl Harbor.

Stella later confirmed that her father was a member of the Rangers, highly skilled Special Forces trained in Oahu prior to being sent to the Philippines and New Guinea. Bud Cunningham died of lung cancer coupled with cirrhosis of the liver. He smoked and drank himself to death. Stella's mother had once confided that, "Dad couldn't erase a terrible memory of bulldozing hundreds of bodies into a mass grave and then pouring kerosene on them for the pyre that would protect from an outbreak of cholera. He could still smell the burning flesh in his nightmares."

Stella was an overly sensitive child, easily upset by loud voices. She heard things she wasn't supposed to hear, as she was a light sleeper. She worried so when her father shouted at her mother about the bills each month. Always, these loud financial discussions happened long after Stella's bedtime.

Bud rarely came home in time to eat dinner with his family. He was a regular at several bars in Oceanside. Stella's mother kept a foil wrapped plate for him most nights, as she knew he needed to eat to slow down the damage of daily drinking. The divorce was initiated by Bud once he learned his mistress was pregnant. The family dynamic went from bad to terrible as Bud transferred his inner rage to Stella, who had defended her mother and refused to accept the new stepmother. Bud was by then a chronic alcoholic.

Stella's time with Doc Z was precious to her. With his help, she came to an understanding of the hurt and suffering that her father endured. For Stella, the phrase that Doc used, "hurt people, hurt people," made perfect sense. She wished she could talk with her father and fix his hurts, but he was gone. Doc Z knew that Stella was a committed Christian and told her to say a special prayer for her father each day and he would surely know of it.

The third walk was organized by Gretchen and her husband Art. It took place at Del Mar Beach at sunset. Gretchen and Art Jackson were the senior members of the Psychological Museum. Doc Z was the best man at their wedding years ago.

Sober and drug free for over 30 years, Gretchen and Art met at an AA meeting in the early 1980s when Gretchen was newly sober and struggling with the reality of living on her own without Jack Daniels, Jose Quervo or Quaalude treats.

Art was the first to speak at the early bird meeting in downtown San Diego. Gretchen was fresh out of rehab and renting a studio apartment near the Federal Courthouse. She was learning to be a court reporter. Gretchen was alone and scared, yet determined to make it. Art's deep voice reminded her of a radio broadcaster. She took notice of his calm yet commanding presence. He wasn't at all her usual dreamboat kind of guy. Art was of medium height and build with a pleasant smile that accompanied quite ordinary looks. He wore his hair in a ponytail and had a short beard. Art rode a Harley and was rarely out of his riding gear. No suit and tie for this dude and better yet, no pensive grimace so often the face of the corporate ass kissers.

"Good morning everyone and welcome to the first morning meeting of Alcoholics Anonymous. I'm Art and I'm an alcoholic celebrating my fifth birthday. I know I look a lot older but five years sober feels good and I am five years into a new and wonderful life. Its not always easy, but then again, my Mom didn't raise any wimps!"

Gretchen sat in the back, not feeling confident enough to interact. It was the first meeting of the day and she had spent a night of tossing and turning. The hot coffee and Art's talk was just what she needed. Art spoke of his party personality and how he dearly loved tying one on with the gang.

"I love drinking! What better way to spend the weekend than with tri-tip BBQ, gallons of beer and shooters, laughing and getting stupid with my pals. Yeah, it was great while it lasted. But when I started the fight that landed four of us in the hospital, I got my first wake up call. I was fired from my job. Did I mention my boss was one of the four? The second wakeup call was when my wife divorced me. The third wake up call was when I felt so sorry for myself that I drank myself into a fog and spent a year in the pokey for causing a five-car pile up that injured six people. I was ordered to get counseling in prison and by golly, it worked."

Gretchen related to the partying but her story was much more dramatic. She wasn't ready to introduce herself to the group and divulge her history of life with a schizophrenic mother, an absent father and her own alcohol and cocaine addiction. Years later, Doc would tell her that her family was textbook material and that all that drama could be a prize winning play like *Who's Afraid of Virginia Wolf?*

Many of the attendees of the first morning meeting frequented the Short Stack Pancake House after the group concluded with the serenity prayer. Art encouraged members to join him, laughing that, "It's not the Bloody Mary that I really want but the pumpkin pancakes are damn good!"

Gretchen went to another meeting later that day. She often went to several meetings in one day. Being alone with her demons and newly sober was more than she could handle. The guest speaker was a barber, sporting a Mohawk and looking every bit like one of the Village People. Something he said midway into his talk resonated with Gretchen.

Vinnie Bellanca, owner of Vinnie's Barber Shop in La Jolla was quite serious as he told his captive audience "Putting my own face forward helps me stay sober. I don't need to follow the instructions of how I should dress, how I should look, how I should do this and how I should do that. Trying to please everybody else was killin' me and I lost myself along the way. I drank for lots of reasons, mainly to fit in with the cool crowd. Then, I got so I liked the highs and hated the hangovers, and we all know the only way to really cure a killer hangover is to guzzle spiked orange juice!"

The crowd laughed and applauded Vinnie. Gretchen knew just what he was talking about. Vinnie told the group that he just about killed himself with drinking.

"I pulled a bender, I mean a real beaut! I paid for it dearly with a nasty case of pancreatitis. Nothing like vomiting blood and bile for days on end to get it through my thick head that I wasn't going to make it if I kept this up."

Vinnie went on to tell the crowd that since he got sober and started having some fun with his own haircuts, his business skyrocketed. "I don't even need to advertise! I just walk around looking like this and wear my Vinnie's Barber Shop T-shirt!" Vinnie then told the group that he gave free haircuts to any "friend of Bill Wilson." That included ladies haircuts.

Gretchen got an idea and acted on it. She introduced herself to Vinnie at the coffee break. "I've been sober for three months. I hate my long hair and I want to re-invent myself."

Vinnie told Gretchen to come to his shop at 6 pm and she would be his last client of the day. He had some ideas.

By 7 pm, Gretchen liked what she saw in the mirror. Vinnie gave her a medium bob cut with well-defined layers. Vinnie's wife, Barb did the make up, using soft pink blush, pink lip gloss and dark brown eye liner that made the most of Gretchen's big blue eyes. Barb gave her a Vinnie's Barber Shop hot pick tank top to wear. Gretchen was on her way to feeling good about her appearance. Vinnie wouldn't let Gretchen pay for a thing. He asked her to promise to keep attending meetings and to stay in touch.

Gretchen was so excited about her new look that she decided to go to the first morning meeting, hoping that she might see Art again. She wore her spandex running pants and her new pink tank top. It was cold that morning so she donned a zip up sweatshirt. She was ready to flirt with Art, given half a chance. But, her new self-image didn't get that half chance to flaunt itself, as Art wasn't in the group.

That morning, Doug addressed the group. "Good Morning. I'm Doug and I'm both an alcoholic and a junkie. You could say I never met a booze or drug I didn't fall in love with." Doug gave a wonderful talk but he wasn't Art. Gretchen sat in the back near the coffee. Just before the break, Art walked in with another guy and took an empty seat next to Gretchen.

"Being somebody's sponsor sometimes means picking them up and getting them to a meeting," said Art. "Tell me what I've missed."

Gretchen was white knuckling her coffee mug, feeling the good vibe and profusely thanking her higher power. "Doug is giving a talk about the double whammy of drinking with drugs. I'm Gretchen and I'm new to this."

"Welcome Gretchen. I'm Art."

Art invited Gretchen to join him and his sober pals to the pancake house. She accepted the invitation. "Oh, I'm starving and could drink about a pot of coffee. I'd love to come but how far is it?"

"It's in Old Town, about three miles from here."

"I'll have to get a taxi. I can't drive for another six months."\

"Yeah! Been there, but, no problem. You can wear my helmet and hop on my Harley with me, that is, if you're not spooked by a motorcycle."

"Hell no, I'm an excitement junkie as well as a drunk!"

Doug finished his talk. The group disbanded. Some of the suits and dresses got into their vehicles and went to work. Others stayed for the next meeting. Gretchen mounted the Harley, held on to Art, again thanking her higher power for a sober rush.

Gretchen told Art the following week that he made her knees weak and made her sweat. He responded that it was too soon for her to jump into a relationship. Art suggested that she attend a weekend sobriety workshop with him. "Its all day Saturday and the workshop is on family dynamics. Everyone gets 15 minutes to present family dreams and nightmares. It's sort of a competition as to who has the most fucked up family. Doc Z is the moderator."

Art told Gretchen all about Doc Z. "He's helped me and I think he might help you. Bottom line, he will help you to help yourself."

A year later, Art and Gretchen married. They volunteered along with Doc at the County Jail and at the Federal Penitentiary at Lompoc. They also took Doc's suggestion that they write a series of plays about their life experiences. Both Art and Gretchen call it their sober work in progress. Now in their late 60's, they perform at every kind of theater, including the prison in Lompoc. Audiences roar with laughter, gasp at the painful tales of abuse and cheer at the triumph of two people who found each other and made life worth living, one day at a time.

Gretchen and Art test out their material while walking with the group at sunset tides, when none of the group members are in a hurry to get somewhere. When suggestions and critiques are over, Gretchen turns on her boom box for the final sober event of the day. She strips to her bikini, gets barefoot and gets down to the Rolling Stones and the sounds of the sixties. The sand- dance floor is full when the CD gets to *Honky Tonk Woman*. Ain't life a beach?

Single Malt Scotch

Publix on Southern Blvd stayed open late during the winter season when so many snowbirds flocked to Palm Beach County. It made for good business and for even better shopping for the twilight bargain hunters.

The deli food was the best deal with the produce coming in at a close second. It was in the fruit section that octogenarian Theresa met Arnie, the man who would turn her world upside down.

While examining the apples for bruises, Theresa Fleming accidentally knocked over the peach display next to the apples. Flustered and embarrassed, Theresa struggled to put the fruit back on the shelves. While doing so, she knocked her grocery cart over and began to cry as the eggs smashed and the watermelon squashed her bread as it splashed red mess everywhere.

Arnie stepped over from the banana section and said, "I always wanted to be knight in shining armor for a damsel in distress!" With that, Arnie got the apples and peaches off the floor and put Theresa's cart upright.

"No need to worry about the mess," Arnie said. "The maintenance crew will take care of it. Let's replace the eggs, watermelon and bread."

Theresa was glad it was late and few shoppers besides Arnie had witnessed her blunder. He was such a lifesaver, this scruffy looking big guy who looked like a linebacker recently sobered up. He wore old khakis and a long sleeve t-shirt with a safari vest. Arnie wasn't particularly good looking but exuded refinement and manners, all things that Theresa put a high value on. Arnie reminded her of one of her favorite students from her teaching days.

"Oh, thank you so very much," said Theresa. "At least my deli food stayed in their containers. I shop late to get the chicken and pasta salad that they would throw out. I get it 75% off don't you know."

No," said Arnie. "I didn't know. If you don't mind, show me where the Deli section is. I'm Arnie."

"I'm Theresa."

Arnie loaded up on chicken wings and carrot salad. The price was right and small containers fit nicely in his satchel. The check out was next and Arnie asked if Theresa needed help with her groceries. He then told her, "A lovely lady like you shopping this late isn't safe."

"Oh, I've never had a bother and I always dress in black to blend in with the night. I saw that on the television show for senior safety. And, just to be extra safe, I always park in the handicapped spot by the door."

"Well, if I want to keep being a knight in shining armor, I'll make sure you get to your car and lock the doors. My truck is by the Publix sign and I can see you from there."

Arnie's pick up was parked a few spots from Theresa's Volvo. He saw her open her trunk and put her bags in. Arnie thought he saw something in the back seat and walked over to check it out. As he got closer, he quickened his pace and pulled his pistol from his inside vest pocket. "Get back inside the store, Ma'am. I got this."

Theresa howled with laughter and told Arnie, "You dear, dear man, its just Fred!" By that time, Arnie had opened the side passenger door and shouted at the slumped over figure, "Get the fuck out of there, you goddam pervert!"

Theresa walked over and introduced Arnie to Fred, the life-sized, anatomically correct inflatable doll that she bought at a garage sale a few years back. "Pleased to meet you Fred, I'm Arnold Mutke."

Arnie put his firearm away and listened as Theresa told him about her $5 purchase that enabled her to drive around at night without worry. She bought second hand clothes for Fred at the Goodwill and changed his outfits with the weather.

"You ever get stopped by a cop?" asked Arnie.

"Oh, my yes, and the West Palm Beach Police know all know Fred. They think I'm a little old lady with a sense of humor."

Arnie said he thought that Fred should sit in the front seat to look more authentic. Theresa told Arnie that most Wednesday nights, she had Verla and Lois with her. Fred shared the back seat with Verla. If they left the car for any length of time, Theresa put a small radio in Fred's lap with the volume on high. Always the country station. It was Verla's idea to stick an empty bottle of Bud between his legs and a stale bag of Doritos next to him.

Both ladies had other plans this night. Theresa explained that Wednesday nights were their weekly outing where they caught the early bird special at Denny's and then took in a movie. They did their grocery shopping afterwards and all were home by midnight. "We love the night!"

With that, Arnie and Theresa bid each other adieux. Arnie told Theresa to drive safely and lock her doors. He drove off in his truck and headed for the mobile home park he called home.

Theresa was in bed and watching Letterman when Lois called to tell her about the board meeting at her condo complex. "That fool resident manager lied through his yellow teeth about improvements at the pool," said Lois. "He said we should all be life guards and scold the careless grandparents who let their grandchildren do cannon balls, scream and run around the pool area and have belching contests."

"He should get fired," said Theresa. "That's what the homeowner's association fee is supposed to pay for! You can't be a pool policewoman! Oh, for Pete's sake!"

"Don't you know it," said Lois. "The kids are dropped off by their parents who go to play golf and then the grandparents bring them to the pool as they can't stand being cooped up with the hellions in a tiny condo. And, to top that off, the grandparents can't swim and most of them are using walkers!"

"All the more reason for me to never downsize! I love my house and I'm never leaving it unless I'm in a coffin," said Theresa.

Theresa then told Lois about her encounter with Arnie. Lois loved hearing about his reaction to Fred. She said that Verla was most likely still up and she would call her to tell her about it. Lois confirmed that the following Wednesday, Theresa would pick them up for their night out. Lois said she hoped Arnie would be there.

Theresa Fleming was known in her neighborhood as an unclaimed treasure. Never married but still beautiful at 83, she taught high school till she was in her seventies. Theresa was a nun from her early twenties till she was thirty. Growing up in a devout Catholic family, young Theresa felt that God had called her for a life of service.

It was in her 27th year, when she met Andrew Lewis, the assistant pastor at St. Patrick's Catholic Church in Kokomo, Indiana. Sister Theresa taught high school English and History at St. Patrick High School. Several of the boys on the football team were behind in their lessons and in danger of getting kicked off the team. Father Lewis, known to all as Father Andy, asked the principal to see if one of the teachers would do some Saturday morning tutoring. Sister Theresa was popular with the students and had the patience to work with the troublesome kids who would rather goof off than study.

The attraction was instant. Father Andy was 34 at the time. Theresa fought her feelings and ignored them as best she could. But, the collaboration of Father Andy helping with the Latin and Sister Theresa helping with the term papers brought them together every Saturday morning during football season. They had intellectual camaraderie and chemistry, a deadly combination for two celibate young people with natural instincts.

The nuns were required to go to Confession every week. Sister Theresa confessed her impure thoughts and poured her heart out. It was Father Andy behind the curtain. He told her that he felt the same about her and that they both needed Divine Guidance.

Theresa's Divine Guidance told her to leave when her mother became ill with cancer. It was the out she needed. Upon her mother's death, Theresa wrote the convent and told them she was never returning. She sold the family home in Indianapolis and took a teaching position in the public school system in West Palm Beach. She bought a little house in the El Cid neighborhood. Sister Theresa was gone and Theresa had moved on.

Two years later, while browsing the religious book section at the local bookstore on Palm Beach, Theresa thought she saw a familiar face. It was Father Andy, in jeans and a t-shirt. She quickly turned her back and put the Mother Theresa book back on the shelf. Too late.

"Theresa, is that you?"

"What on earth are you doing in Florida?"

"I'm the pastor at a church in Sebastian. Just came down here for the day. I've thought about you often. How are you?"

They went for coffee and talked for hours. Theresa promised to drive north and meet Andy for lunch the following Wednesday. They met in Vero Beach and had a picnic, so as not to bump into any parishioners at local restaurants.

It all happened so fast. Andy had every Wednesday off and was free on Sunday afternoons after the Masses were said. Theresa rented a studio apartment in Vero Beach and they began their love affair.

Once a year, Andy went on a two week driving vacation. He told everyone that he wanted to see the National Parks and commune with nature. Theresa joined him. They were careful but not careful enough. Theresa became pregnant. Both were thrilled but fearful of ruining Andy's career in the Church. Andy's cousin was a doctor in Port St. Lucie and aware of the situation. She accepted Theresa as her new patient and delivered baby Micah Fleming. Theresa took an extended maternity leave and stayed at the apartment so Andy could visit frequently.

Andy's career was on the upswing. When Micah was 14 months old, Andy was sent to Rome to complete a four-week immersion study on Vatican policy regarding homosexuals. It was during this absence from Florida that Micah became ill with haemophilus meningitis. Theresa was frantic. Micah had a raging fever and was in isolation at Children's Hospital.

Calls to Andy went unanswered as he was in study all day. Micah died, shattering Theresa. Andy returned and joined Theresa in overwhelming grief.

Andy had his work and his belief that Micah was with God. Theresa was despondent and questioned her faith and her love for Andy. Was God punishing them? Andy feared that Theresa would take her own life. He also feared that their love for each other was irreparably damaged.

It was the doctor who delivered Micah who told Theresa that she had to choose if her life were better with Andy or without him. She chose life with Andy. They had twenty years of their secret relationship when Andy succumbed to an aneurysm. He was then a Bishop with an impeccable reputation. Theresa didn't attend the funeral. Her consolation was that Micah was now with his father.

Theresa was now in her senior years and hoped to be reunited with her loves soon. Meantime, she kept life interesting for Lois and Verla.

Lois Andersen moved to Florida after the death of her husband Randall ten years ago. Verla divorced her cheating second husband, left Cincinnati and moved to Florida, paying cash for her Palm Vista condo. She lost her driver's license while driving the wrong way on Military Trail at rush hour. Verla never had children. Now 80, Verla used a cane and firmly believed most any conspiracy theory on corrupt Republicans. She met Theresa and Lois when they each volunteered for the Haitian Earthquake Relief.

Lois spent her entire life in Kenosha, Wisconsin. Randall was her college sweetheart. He made a comfortable living as a manager of a hardware store. They had one child, a plastic surgeon with a thriving practice in Boca Raton.

Dr. Jonathan Andersen was the darling of the boob job set. He was handsome, polished and loved to sail and drink expensive wine. Keeping the ladies looking young kept his wallet full. Having his mother around cramped his style. To make sure that he would be free of intrusion, he purchased a condo for her in Wellington, a thirty-minute drive from Boca.

As Lois didn't drive anymore, it made for an easy once a month visit, when his schedule permitted.

Lois was bored and eager to make new friends. She was not fooled by her only child's selfish ways and had long accepted the fact that he would never fill his father's shoes. Dr. Jonathan made more money than his father, had more cars and toys, and even a prettier wife, but he lacked the compassion and moral compass of his father.

When Lois met Theresa and Verla, they found that they had much in common. They loved to read, to play bridge and backgammon and each refused to go willingly into old age. They loved the night and loved adventure. Lois had insisted that Theresa get Fred for their escort. It was Lois who pulled out the five-dollar bill at the garage sale. "Oh my God! This guy could be our evening escort with no strings attached!"

Fred was naked when they bought him. Theresa deflated him and tossed him into the trunk. Lois called Verla and asked what she was doing that night. "Verla, if you aren't otherwise engaged, Theresa will come and get you and we can have some Kentucky Fried Chicken and play pinochle."

Evenings such as this were overnights for Lois and Verla. All three ladies enjoyed gin and tonics for their happy hour and shared a bottle of wine with their evening meal. Once they had their chicken dinner, Theresa said that she needed some help with inflating an automobile ornament. With fits of giggling and much effort, Fred grew into his manhood.

"We've got to get him some clothes," said Verla.

"Tomorrow is senior discount day at Goodwill. Let's get him some outfits."

Together, the ladies found jeans, sneakers and Gators sweat shirts for Fred to wear. They also picked up a few t-shirts and flip-flops. Fred's toes were rather chubby so they bought the largest size they could find. For Verla, a woman twice divorced, Fred took on the role of the perfect boyfriend. Fred was always there and never, ever said an unkind word.

On evenings out, Verla enjoyed placing Fred's hand on her knee, shrieking, "Fred! You naughty boy!" Lois took her cue and told Verla that she was a senior slut and that poor old Fred was vulnerable to her promiscuity.

Arnie was another story altogether. Originally from Crystal City, Missouri, Arnie (really Karl) was the orphaned son of Joyce and Richard Miller. Joyce succumbed to breast cancer four years after Richard was killed in Desert Storm. Karl was 16 and spent his remaining young years with his maternal grandmother. He joined the Air Force after graduating Washington University in St. Louis.

Granny Krug was a highborn Berliner and spoke all the European languages. Karl enjoyed the daily games of speaking different languages at every meal. Granny Krug was also a left over asset of the American Government. Her contributions to defeating Hitler included coaching American spies in dialects, cultural customs and poisoning techniques. Granny was a marvelous cook.

Young Karl missed his parents terribly. Granny took a pragmatic approach to preparing her grandson for the world at large. She taught him everything she knew, thus making Karl a secret weapon.

Karl loved airplanes. When Karl was in his senior year, Granny told him if he brought home a straight A report card, she would give him a series of flying lessons for his 18th birthday. Karl negotiated an even better promise. If he continued to get straight A's, then Granny would keep Karl enrolled in flight training. By the time Karl joined the Air Force, he had his multi-engine instrument license, helicopter license and thousands of hours of flight time. He took foreign languages and international commerce at Washington University, maintaining his A's.

The ultimate thrill for a flyboy was to learn to fly fighter jets. He joined the Air Force shortly after graduation. The military offered adventure in the sky with a touch of discipline thrown in, which Karl didn't appreciate. The Air Force exploited Karl's ability in the cockpit, sending him on missions where his skill was needed. Problems surfaced when Karl was bored.

Karl enjoyed his beer with shots of Jagermeister and a good fight in any language necessary. He had yet to mature enough to keep his mouth shut when he disagreed with his superiors. Let's just say that Karl was never a yes man. He got away with a lot of insubordination as he was of great value to the ongoing fight to preserve freedom. His missions were off the books, often at night and often picking up questionable people and things.

It was on one of these helicopter night flights that Karl saw the light. His own government was participating in the drugs and guns business. Iran Contra paled in comparison to what Karl witnessed. His grumblings and refusal to fly more missions earned him the threat of court martial. He agreed to one more mission.

Karl flew under the radar and landed on a deserted country road in Northern Turkey. He changed his clothes, leaving all of Karl Miller behind and then blew up the helicopter. A new life awaited Arnold Mutke.

Arnie grew a beard and let his hair grow. He bought some cheap hair color and turned his light brown locks and beard to black. He bought a bicycle and blended into the countryside. He soon found work as a cook on a fishing boat. Granny's recipes came in handy. Arnie's biscuits and seafood chowder were the best the crew had ever tasted. They kept him busy, as their appetites were ravenous after hours of hard work.

While at sea in mid May, Arnie made some special sauce for the freshly caught grouper. He also made extra biscuits so the men could sop up plenty of the sauce. The Captain and entire crew slept a full 12 hours before awakening the next morning. Arnie was gone with the small boat and all their cash and valuables.

Granny received a letter postmarked from Normandy, France. Granny called in a few favors and soon Arnie had a passport and was on the way to Florida. Granny followed a few months later. She bought a mobile home and hired Arnold Mutke as a handyman and live in helper. Granny called in a few more favors and made sure that Arnold Mutke had a valid social security number and an established bank account. They lived very comfortably on her social security benefits and Arnie's day trading earnings. Granny brought the two gold bars she had hidden in her basement since the forties. Granny made Arnie promise that the bars were never to be used for frivolous things. They were to be used only for medical emergencies and for exit strategies. Granny's view of the world was realistic.

Now that Arnie knew the secrets of late night bargain shopping at Publix, he made sure to shop between 10 and midnight when his favorites were wonderfully discounted. Theresa made his day with her buddy Fred and Arnie hoped he would bump into her again. His affinity for older ladies made him feel connected to Granny. She had been gone now for three years. Arnie still missed her but knew her life had been full. Raising him after the death of her only child kept her going. Arnie knew that he had made her proud with his refusal to participate in the skullduggery of dirty politics. Granny always said that she was a sucker for a bad ass.

Arnie heard them before he saw them. The tribe of excitement junkies was going through the household products, calculating the deals on toilet paper. Verla forgot her hearing aid and Lois and Theresa had to shout at her.

Arnie walked over to the cleaning products aisle and whistled. Theresa looked up and Arnie waved. "There's my knight in shining armor," said Theresa. With that, Lois gave the come over sign to Verla. They joined Theresa. "Girls, say hello to Arnie," said Theresa.

It was love at first sight for both Lois and Verla. Arnie was in his Jimmy Buffet attire. He showed off his athletic build and tan with his shorts and sleeveless t-shirt. Arnie was the perfect grandson they never had.

Arnie agreed to join them for ice cream at a diner a few blocks down Southern Blvd. Always the gentleman, Arnie walked them to Theresa's Volvo and put their bags in the trunk. He said hello to Fred.

Lois and Theresa shared a banana split, Arnie got a butterscotch sundae and Verla had her favorite peppermint ice cream on top of a fudge brownie. No one counted calories anymore. While enjoying their ice cream, each shared their minute biography. Arnie told them that he left the Chicago

Fire Department after ten years on the job. He said the stress of being a firefighter took its toll on his health. He loved the ocean and the cold Chicago winters were just too harsh. He took a course in investing and made a living doing day trading. He lived modestly for now, but shared with the ladies, that he longed to buy a boat and live on it. Arnie also shared with the ladies that he liked fishing off the Lake Worth Pier.

"If you get a grouper or a snapper, let me know," said Theresa. "I've got a bar b q on my patio and we could have a real Florida feast."

"I'll do that," said Arnie. "Grouper is my favorite eating fish."

Lois spoke up and said that she had too much food in her freezer and needed to have a dinner party for the group to eat it. Verla said she would bring the wine. Lois gave the group a choice of pot roast or chicken. They voted on the pot roast. Arnie said he could come over early and transform the pot roast into sauerbraten, make German potato salad and biscuits from scratch. They set the date for the following Sunday.

Arnie wowed them with his German cuisine. Theresa suggested to Lois and Verla that they adopt Arnie as Fred's brother. They agreed and Arnie let himself become one of the tribe.

Life was good for the next several months. Arnie gave them stock tips and excellent companionship. Verla especially enjoyed Arnie's commentaries on political conspiracies. What was not to love about Arnie? He supplied freshly caught seafood, fixed things in their homes, and supplied authentic dirty clothes for Fred. Lois loved this as she said it reminded her of the way Randall smelled when he returned from his hunting trips with the Knights of Columbus and wanted sex.

It had been over twelve years since Karl Miller went missing and was presumed dead. Karl was never too far from Arnie though and Karl had a photographic memory.

One evening at sunset as Arnie was getting his gear out of his truck for some twilight fishing, he saw a familiar face walking along the Lake Worth Beach, just across from the golf course. It was one of the men Karl Miller had extracted from a clandestine transaction in Algeria. The guy was a total prick and Karl never forgot his lack of respect. He treated Karl like a cab driver and told Karl's commanding officer that he was treated badly by Karl, who had called him a motherfucker in his own language and then spit on him. The prick smelled of whiskey and dirty money.

Karl didn't like what he had seen as the prick ran towards the rescue helicopter. No witnesses. Hard to prove that Karl wasn't polite but the commanding officer knew better. Karl couldn't go drinking with his flyboys for a month and was again threatened with court martial.

Now, this same prick was taking a stroll with a blonde on Arnie's beach. Might be interesting to find out what the prick was up to these days. Arnie looked like a bum and had a pail full of bloody chum for bait. He decided to confirm his suspicions. Arnie waited till the pair was near the pier. Arnie walked up to them,

"Hey man, you got any spare change for some coffee? Ah could sure use a cup while I fish for my supper."

The well-groomed man pulled the blonde close and told Arnie that he was vermin and to get lost. The accent was the same and the guy was still a prick. Arnie walked to the pier and cast his line. He had some serious thinking to do.

Arnie had a good night, catching a pompano and two snappers. He formulated a plan of action. After cleaning the fish and popping them on ice in the cooler, Arnie got to work researching the prick.

Thomas Schmidt was a registered guest at the Four Seasons Resort. Karl knew his real name was Raf Shevers. Thomas Schmidt was a geologist specializing in rare gems. He was brought to Palm Beach to appraise the jewels of a recently deceased billionaire. Raf Shevers was a whore for anyone willing to pay his price for trafficking weapons and children. It didn't sit well with Karl that Raf was still enjoying life.

Several hours of research later, Arnie determined that Karl had some unfinished business to attend to. But before Karl could get to work, Arnie had promised to drop off the freshly caught fish at Theresa's. "Can't make it for the bar b q tonight," said Arnie. "Give my best to Lois and Verla."

Theresa was no fool and knew something was bothering Arnie. She was worried about him. He had wormed his way into her heart. Maternal instincts never leave. Theresa knew where Arnie lived and made a plan. She called Lois and Verla and changed the bar b q to the following Sunday. The fish went into her freezer.

One of Theresa's former students was a private investigator in Deerfield Beach. She called him and asked what he could do for her for $500. "I can't really afford more than that," said Theresa. "But this dear young man is in some kind of trouble and I want to make sure he is all right."

"No problem, Miss Fleming," said Adam Bader. 'I've got a team in West Palm that can track his comings and goings. Send me all the information you have on him."

Theresa didn't have much to email besides the stories that Arnie had told her. She knew where he lived as he told her it was a mobile home park a few miles from the Publix on Southern. Within a few hours, Adam called Theresa to say that there was no record of Arnold Mutke ever working for the Chicago Fire Department. Adam warned Theresa to stay clear of Arnold Mutke as he was not who he said he was. The surveillance team reported that Arnold Mutke never left his mobile home for the two days that they watched him.

Theresa said to stop the investigation, as she couldn't afford more. Adam told her to notify the police if she felt threatened in any way, then cautioned her to cut ties with whoever Arnold Mutke really was.

Theresa was beside herself and had to talk to Lois and Verla about it. They concurred that they should take matters into their own hands and confront Arnie. They would do this over ice cream on Wednesday night.

Arnie left a message for Thomas Schmidt at the Four Seasons, inviting him to a private viewing of gold coins found by divers in Key West. Arnie also included a coded reference for the acquisition of weapons. The viewing would be at the Holiday Inn on South Ocean Ave in Delray Beach at 7 that evening. Bearers bonds and precious gems were the accepted currency. The message asked for an email confirmation. Schmidt emailed his confirmation immediately upon getting the message.

Arnie got into his truck at 3:30 and went directly to the bait shop. He bought what he needed for some late night fishing. Then, he headed on 95 and went to Delray. He parked his truck a few blocks away from the Holiday Inn.

Arnie walked over to the men's rest room at the Delray Beach and changed into his khaki's and Hawaiian shirt. He stuffed his fishing attire into his leather briefcase. Arnie walked over to the liquor store and purchased a bottle of the single malt scotch whiskey that Raf was known to drink. He then walked over to the Beachcomber Deli and bought cheese and some fresh fruit.

At six, Arnie went to the front desk of the Holiday Inn and asked that Mr. Schmidt meet his party at the ocean view room that Sam Gabbone had reserved. Arnie took the stairs to the room and waited for his prey. At 6:50, Thomas Schmidt read his message and took the elevator to the top floor. He knocked on the door of Room 313 and Sam Gabbone answered it with a cheerful greeting in his Texas drawl. "Welcome, Mr. Schmidt. Let's have a drink and then do sum binis."

Raf saw the briefcase on the bed and saw his brand of single malt on the patio table. Arnie poured him a glass and offered him some brie and grapes. Raf eagerly drank his glass of scotch. Arnie munched on a cracker topped with brie and watched as Raf got dizzy.

Arnie spoke quietly, using Raf's mother tongue telling him that what goes around comes around and the payback can be a real bitch. Raf stumbled into the room and passed out. Arnie poured a generous amount of scotch on Raf and put a bag of high-grade heroin in his pocket. He then took his wallet and opened Raf's briefcase and took the bearer bonds and gems he brought for the potential transaction. Arnie changed into his fishing clothes.

Arnie left using the stairs. He drove directly to the Lake Worth Pier and went fishing, as was his customary Sunday evening activity. Once his line was in the water, Arnie used a burner phone to text a message to the Palm Beach County Sheriff that a drug deal was going down at the Delray Holiday Inn. He gave the room number.

Thomas Schmidt awakened in the hospital. With no identity, the police fingerprinted him and found that Raf Shevers was wanted in several countries for human trafficking and money laundering. He was appointed a public defender and awaited his trial.

Arnie was happy. Raf was not. He recognized the voice from long ago and asked his attorney to negotiate a deal for him. Hard to do when all the information that Raf could supply was that an AWOL Air Force Pilot was somewhere in Florida.

Karl had been careful, but Arnie was out of practice. He left fingerprints on the doorknob at the Holiday Inn. The next day, Karl Miller's photo was on the news with an artist's enhancement of what he might look like now. Verla saw it first and called Theresa. "It's Arnie! I just know it. Turn your TV on!"

Theresa was stunned. It was beyond belief. She couldn't let anything happen to Arnie. Theresa got into her Volvo and drove to the mobile home park where she knew that Arnie lived. It was past midnight. He too had seen the news and was packing his satchel to leave. Theresa pounded on his door.

"Theresa! What are you doing here?"

"Did you see the news? You're a wanted man."

Arnie didn't have time to explain his past to Theresa. He had to get going before the manager of the mobile home park called in with information on Karl Miller. There was a reward attached to the successful apprehension.

"I've got a plan," said Theresa. "I threw Fred in the trunk. Get in my car and be quiet while I get us back to my house."

Arnie threw his laptop into his satchel after hitting send. He had used bill pay on his online banking to donate his remaining cash to the ASPCA. Arnie had already packed his stash of bearer bonds and gems that he had taken from Raf and Granny's gold bars.

They were out the door and into Theresa's garage by 12:30. Fred was returned to the front seat and Arnie was safely inside the house. Now what? Theresa didn't know whether to cry or laugh. Arnie was stressed.

Theresa called Lois and Verla and told them that she would pick them up the following day for their overnight dinner party. She told each to bring some cash. They would go to the Goodwill to get some new clothes for Fred.

That night, Arnie held court at the dining room table. He confessed his past. The ladies were proud of him and said they would come up a solution. A few months later, Arnie had a new identity, a new boat and new fishing gear.

Lois took the gems to her son in Boca. He put them in his safety deposit box with the promise that each year, he would have a jeweler make a lovely pendant for his mother. If she died, the pendant would go to either Theresa or Verla. She also guilted him into removing Arnie's fingerprints with acid and giving Arnie a nose job and full lips. Theresa's kitchen was the operating room. Lois reluctantly told her son that he could use one of the rubies as payment.

Dr. Jonathan also supplied a prosthetic bra for Arnie to wear when he was Ardith Anne. The ladies went to Macy's and bought full coverage make-up, depilatory cream and a lovely wardrobe for Ardith Anne just prior to their cruise to Puerto Rico.

Ardith Anne met friends of her grandmother's family in San Juan. She notified the cruise ship that she wouldn't be on board for the return to Florida. Raf never had another drop of single malt scotch and perished in a jailhouse brawl while awaiting trial. Three times each year, the ladies go on a cruise, always somewhere new and always somewhere warm where the fishing is excellent.

Cosmopolitans

Delicious, dangerous, and deadly! Cosmopolitans were the favorite drink of the Dakota Divas. The thirty something gals from Sioux Falls got together once a month to visit, trash husbands or current boyfriends, and to give each other career or parenting advise, depending on the job. They all agreed that parenting was the most difficult and paid the least in dollars and the most in love.

The young mothers envied the career gals for their freedom, their involvement in the business world, and their chic wardrobes. The career gals longed for a loving husband and a baby.

The Divas rotated houses on the last Friday of the month. They each contributed to the meal and everyone helped with clean up. The hostess of the evening provided the main dish and dessert.

The drinks were made by the expert Kyla, who had put herself through law school as a bartender at the Jury Pool, an upscale bar close to South Dakota State Law School. Kyla was the favorite bartender at the Jury Pool as she never skimped on the ingredients and knew that just a touch more triple sec made all the difference. Kyla was also gorgeous and six feet tall with endless legs.

Louise was hosting this late April evening. The weather was cooperating with a clear and starry night. Kyla arrived first and made the pitcher of their favorite cocktail. Louise suggested they sit outside and watch the sunset. Kyla poured them each a glass.

"So, tell me about your day," said Kyla

"Boring but productive as I cleaned, shopped for groceries and made the pies," said Louise. "Tell me something I can get excited about....let me live vicariously as a kick ass chick lawyer in court."

Kyla worked in the largest law firm in Sioux Falls. She paid her dues by doing endless research and document reviews, while lobbying for courtroom time. She was quickly gaining a well-earned reputation as a litigation star. Kyla loved the courtroom and most juries loved Kyla. As a child, Kyla was known as the great pretender in her family, assuming the role of a princess, a pink fairy, a mermaid and as she grew into adolescence and teens, a dancer, a rock star and the ultimate drama queen.

Attorney at Law Kyla had the commanding presence of a seasoned council, with a gentle and disarming demeanor. Kyla's voice and looks could have just as easily earned her a place on network television. Opposing council called her sneaky and feared her. They also loved the chance to do battle with her.

"I spent the entire day working on witness questions and strategy. My head hurts just thinking about it," said Kyla.

"What kind of trial is it," asked Louise.

"This one's a real estate nightmare," said Kyla. "The new owners of a house in a new subdivision are suing the builders and the real estate company for failing to disclose a serious health hazard. Seems there had been a nasty mold problem that wasn't completely resolved before the new owners moved in. Their oldest child was in remission from leukemia and his immune system was weakened by the chemo....and he got sick within the first week of their taking occupancy."

Louise put her hands to her face. "Oh my God, did the little boy die?"

"No, the doctors couldn't figure it out at first, but one of the nurses had just watched a show about the hidden dangers of a strain of mold that can kill you. She mentioned it to the doctor. The tests proved it and the mother and child had to take their clothes off immediately, take showers at the hospital, wear borrowed scrubs and go to a motel. The house was examined for hazardous materials and my firm now has one hum dinger of a law suit."

The doorbell rang and Louise got up to greet Allison, Stephanie and Lynn. Stephanie brought the Caesar salad, Lynn had the hummus and Allison brought home made bread. Lynn worked in a bank. Allison was an account executive in a public relations firm. Stephanie was a full time Mom with a five year old and a two year old.

"I couldn't find the croutons that I usually use for the salad," said Stephanie. "So, I got creative and took some sour dough bread and made my own....hope you like them as I might have put a touch too much garlic in with the Parmesan."

"Hey, this is a girls night, who cares if we reek of garlic," responded Allison.

They all laughed and raised their glasses to the best ever salad.

Louise made butternut squash lasagna in deference to Lynn, the most ardent of animal lovers in the group. Lynn went vegetarian after learning the cruel facts of animal life in a carnivorous society. Allison made her own version of Parmesan bread, which was the old stand by of basic beer bread with lots and lots of fresh grated Parmesan cheese from the deli.

The divas enjoyed the last hour of twilight, feeling the lovely buzz of the Cosmopolitans and the security of good friends. Louise had set the timer for 60 minutes, the optimum time for her signature lasagna to cook slowly so the cheese would be gooey and the squash blended perfectly.

"Give me about five minutes and when you hear the bell, come and get it!"

Louise had set the dining room table with her good china and crystal and silver flatware. Life was so hurried and scheduled for all the divas that a night of elegance, blended with laughter and stimulating conversation gave them each a chance to feel special. It was Lynn who started the tradition when she surprised the divas at their first gathering at her home. "Why save my finest for special occasions and la de da relatives? Who's better than us divas?"

Louise's husband Keith approved of the diva nights as it gave him a chance to hang out with his buddies or to work late without feeling guilty about it. When it was Louise's hostess night, he surprised her with a few bottles of good wine. Tonight, Louise was serving a wonderful *pinot noir* that Keith had a case of, compliments of one of his customers at his auto dealership.

The meal was delicious and the conversation was even better. Kyla held mock court, telling the divas about her mold case and how she would play up to the jury, sure to include a few parents. She entertained with her ability to turn on the mean girl interrogator and easily switch to the maternal and emotional sympathizer.

"So, Kyla, are there any hot lawyers working the other side of this case?" asked Lynn.

"No, the other side are all geezers from the most expensive law firm in the city. And to be honest, I don't want another lawyer to snuggle up with. Give me a doctor, an architect or better yet, a millionaire business man with his own jet!"

Lynn, the promiscuous one of the divas chimed in with,

"Amen to that, I could go for a guy with money about now."

"Selective...that's the word of the night," said Allison. "My cousins Gary and Todd might be the perfect double dates for you two."

Allison proceeded to tell the Divas that her two cousins on her mother's side were bachelors with that blend of bad boy and over achiever, making them the perfect storms for Divas looking for an exciting challenge.

"Get this! My cousin Gary went to law school, graduated Magna Cum Laude and then changed his mind about being a lawyer. My Uncle Bill had put him through law school and was really counting on a family attorney when Gary decides that he will join his younger brother in medicine."

Kyla was now more than interested.

"So, set me up with one of these cousins of yours. I love both of them already."

Stephanie asked about their sex appeal.

"So, Ali! Describe the cousins. Are they good looking?"

"Hey, they're my cousins and my family doesn't have anyone less than a ten in the gene pool! Gary has baby blue eyes, dark hair, stands 6'3" and lifts weights. Anyone want to know about his looks? Eye candy of course! Todd has brown eyes, also lifts weights and could be Johnny Depp's long lost twin, and yes

Lynn, I would bet big money that he knows how to keep his women smiling."

Louise brought out the ice cream pies, a Diva favorite concoction of chocolate pie crust, vanilla soft ice cream topped with whipped cream and chocolate syrup.

"Oh yum, give me a big piece of that pie," said Stephanie. "I'm not counting calories tonight!"

The empty wine glasses were replaced with aperitif glasses filled with Triple Sec. Louise poured hers over her slice of pie as did Stephanie. Kyla poured half of hers into her Cosmopolitan glass and half on top of her pie. The integration of all the flavors pleased the divas so much that they were silent for a full two minutes save for the moaning of approval. Kyla was the leanest of the divas and ate a second slice of pie, and popped another shot of Triple Sec on top.

"Good Lord! How can you eat that much and drink that much and stay skinny?" asked Louise.

"I'll burn this off during the trial, and hey, I don't want to hurt anyone's feelings by ignoring this glorious food!"

Diva dinner conversation concluded and the clean up took less than twenty minutes. A group effort insured Louise that she wouldn't face a mess in the morning. The dishes were washed, dried and put back in the china cabinet. The crystal and silver, also carefully washed by hand, were back in their safe places.

"Anyone need a taxi?" asked Keith, who had just walked in. "I'm free and I haven't had a drop. I had to work my ass off while you girls were having all the fun."

"Did you eat anything?" asked Louise.

Keith shook his head.

"I can fix you a plate of lasagna but we ate all the salad," said Louise.

"Whatever is left over, I'll finish it off. I'm starved, but first things first. Any diva need a ride home?"

"I thought ahead," said Stephanie. "Jed drove us over and I just called him to pick us up. We are having a pajama party tonight with chick flix and pancakes in the morning guaranteed to cure any hangovers. "

All the divas, save Kyla left their cars at Stephanie's house and accepted her husband's offer to play cabbie. They each collected their corning ware and Pyrex bowls, grabbed their coats and gave goodbye air kisses.

"How about you Kyla?" asked Keith.

"Hey, I could drink you all under the table. Thanks, but no. I need my car first thing in the morning."

"Offer stands till I get my first beer. And if you get pulled over, don't blame me."

Kyla cornered Allison as they were walking out.

"Hey, I could sure use a little romance in my life about now. Please have one of your cousins call me."

"I already texted Todd your cell," said Allison.

"So, what else did you text him about me?"

"I kept it pithy."

"What's that supposed to mean?"

"Just the basics...gorgeous and horny... and then your phone number."

" Oh Lord, I hope he has a sense of humor!"

Kyla then drove off in her Smart Car, careful to keep the speed limit as she knew the consequences of getting pulled over. At this point in her career, she couldn't afford a stain on her reputation.

Kyla was just about back to her condo when her phone buzzed with the alert that a text had arrived. She was anxious to see if it was from Todd. It was and message was short and to the point.

"Hey Beautiful! Coffee tomorrow? When and Where?"

Kyla smiled, and as she was thumbing her reply, slammed into the beautiful old oak tree at the entrance to her building. The Smart Car was totaled. Kyla's neck was broken. When the police found her cell phone, she had typed "Hi ther"